First published in 2019 by Sharpe Books

Siege

RICHARD FOREMAN

"Faith is to believe what you do not see; the reward of this faith is to see what you believe."

St Augustine.

SIEGE

"Faith is to believe what you do not see; the reward of this faith is to see what you believe."
St Augustine.

1.

"You may call yourself a knight, but you are no nobleman," Girard of Mortain scornfully asserted, after forcing his English opponent back again. The high-born Norman wore a clean woollen surcoat – white, with a red cross sewn below his left shoulder – underneath an expensive suit of mail. His boots were made from Italian leather. His practice sword – the edges and point blunted – was forged from Spanish steel. The young man's fine features – strong jaw, aquiline nose – had been burnished by the Mediterranean sun over the course of the long, arduous pilgrimage. Like many noblemen - who had answered Pope Urban II's call to fight the enemies of God and re-take the Holy City of Jerusalem – Girard was a second son, largely disinherited by his elder sibling. The knight had taken the cross in the hope of saving his soul – and making his fortune in the process. He dreamed of one day returning to his province, riding out in front of a mighty company of men upon a coal-black destrier - and disinheriting his brother.

Girard's sneer unfurled itself into a triumphant smile. He licked the sweat from his upper lip, as if he were licking off the wine he would drink, that his uncle Raymond of Toulouse promised him, for winning the contest, against Bohemond of Taranto's man. And winning would prove easier than the nobleman first thought. As per his lord's instructions Girard aimed to toy with his opponent, before ending the bout. Victory would come from a competitor yielding - or being knocked unconscious.

"By embarrassing the Englishman, you will, in turn, be embarrassing his paymaster. And that will bring me no small portion of pleasure," Raymond had remarked with a wolfish grin, sitting on his throne-like iron chair in the main chamber of his billet.

Girard advanced once more and unleashed a flurry of attacks, which the Englishman was barely able to deflect with his chipped second sword and battered second shield.

"You should have remained on your pox-ridden island, Englishman – eating your shit food and enjoying your drear weather. You could be now back in your hovel there, ploughing one of your bow-legged women – as my countrymen once ploughed through your lands during the Harrying of the North."

The Norman spat out his words with relish. He hoped to goad his opponent into making a mistake, as well as garner a few laughs from his supporters.

The Englishman – Edward Kemp – appeared too breathless to reply, even though the veteran campaigner could speak French as fluently as his native tongue. The cross on his threadbare jerkin, beneath a second-hand mail shirt, had faded. His weathered features betrayed his weary spirit. To some observers, Kemp owned a beleaguered air of defeat before he even picked up his sword.

Cheers and jeers buffeted his ears in equal measure, from the crowd which encircled the two combatants. Knights looked on – as well as attendants, farriers, armourers and infantrymen – enjoying the entertainment. It was better that just two men fought against each other - in a proxy fight between Raymond and Bohemond - than two rival armies. The pilgrims doubtless appreciated the distraction. The fire in their bellies, as they urged their respective champions on, made them temporarily forget about their hunger. They feasted on the spectacle, albeit some half-watched whilst they feverishly placed wagers on the outcome.

Kemp's face was sunburnt rather than burnished. His cropped, dusty brown hair was marked with several small scars, picked up from tavern brawls and battlefields alike. His nose had been broken more times than a troubadour's heart. A few grey hairs coloured the forty-five-year old's unkempt beard. The soldier's eyes were a deep hazel. At night, they appeared black. As black as his soul, the soldier would half-joke.

The other Englishman present, Thomas Devin, winced for his countryman as Girard used his sword as a hammer, striking it against the anvil of Kemp's splintering shield. Thomas served in Bohemond's retinue too, as a scribe and translator. The studious youth had an innocent face – and an innocent heart. Thomas had stood in the crowd on that fateful day in Clermont, when Pope Urban II had called upon Christendom to liberate the Holy City from the infidel. The well-read son of a wealthy wool merchant had journeyed to France to further his studies and visit the famed monastery at Cluny. But Urban – or God even – had touched his soul. For once in his life, the student experienced a sense of purpose. Meaning. Grace abounded. He knew he needed to step beyond the threshold of his village and his father's library. A divine wind fed his sails. Thomas had prayed that night in Clermont and reverently uttered the word as if it were the name of his first love:

Jerusalem.

The adolescent's smooth face was now wrinkled with worry, however. He was fearful of his friend suffering an injury. Edward's pride would doubtless be wounded too, should he finish second-best in the contest. The knight had been teaching Thomas how to fight – and in return the young scholar had been teaching Edward how to read. Surprisingly, or not, it was the older man who was progressing in his new field of study more than the youth.

Thomas noticed Edward glance at Owen, a Welsh archer, who was a close companion of the English knight. Owen possessed a roguish expression and a roguish heart. The compactly built soldier was one of the finest bowmen in Bohemond's company, even when half drunk. Months of near starvation had failed to re-sculpture his barrel chest and muscular arms. The archer shook his head at the swordsman, perhaps in disappointment or to convey to his friend to yield and stop the bout, before suffering serious impairment, Thomas considered.

The afternoon sun beat down on the ground like a smouldering fist, seemingly dissolving any wisps of cloud in the azure sky like fat being burned in a pan. A horse whinnied in the background, over the babbling noise of the crowd, letting its owner know that it was as hungry as any other poor creature in the camp.

Looming large behind the two combatants, an island in a sea of mountains and marshland was the city of Antioch – with its steep walls and multiple turrets, which jutted out like boastful chins. The city the pilgrims had besieged for over six months, since their arrival in October. The western armies had almost surrounded Antioch and its various gates. *Almost.* The Turkish governor, Yaghi Siyan, had been able to smuggle provisions in to feed the city. He had even sent out troops to attack Frankish foraging parties. The city stood as defiantly now as it did in October. Perhaps even more defiantly, as despair now eclipsed hope for the pilgrims. A mighty Saracen army, led by Kerbogha of Mosul, was marching to relieve Antioch and defeat the westerners.

"The Army of God has turned into the army of God Help Us," Edward had sardonically remarked to the devout young scribe, whilst he prepared himself for the contest against Raymond's chosen man.

"God will not abandon us," Thomas had replied, faithfully. Hopefully. He clutched the silver crucifix around his neck as he spoke. God had been with them at Clermont, at the siege of Nicaea and the Battle of Dorylauem. The Christian sincerely believed that God would not forsake them now, at Antioch.

"Abandon us? I doubt the bastard was ever with us in the first place," Edward countered, before downing a cup of wine and poking a new notch into his belt with his dagger, from where his waist had shrunk again.

As much as Thomas was growing accustomed to his friend's sacrilegious outbursts, he still blanched and silently said a quick prayer to counteract the cynical knight's blasphemy.

The youth prayed for his companion once more. Not to win the contest (as he felt he may be asking too much of God for that). But to just survive the encounter, without suffering any perilous wounds.

Girard attacked, almost dancing forward. Posturing. Swords clanged together, setting Thomas' teeth on edge. The Norman thought how pleased his old fencing master would be with his technique. The young warrior had yet to be truly tested in battle, having been ill, conveniently or not, or absent during previous engagements. But he would make a name for himself by defeating Bohemond's champion.

The Englishman winced and let out a curse, as a minor gash on his right hip - picked up from a Turkish blade during an ambush when accompanying a foraging party - opened-up.

"Age has finally caught up with him, I warrant," Godfrey of Bouillon said, standing just behind Robert of Flanders. "Edward would have easily bested this pup in his prime."

"I wouldn't write the Englishman off quite yet. An old lion is still a lion," Robert replied, knowingly and equitably. Adhemar spoke highly of the soldier, and Robert thought highly of the bishop.

Half the crowd let out a gasp – and half a cheer – as Girard's blade swept past Edward's face, narrowly missing his nose. Dust puffed up from the ground as the ageing knight shuffled backwards. He sighed in relief, or exhaustion.

Edward flittingly gazed at Owen. The Welsh archer this time subtly nodded to his companion. The bowman had finally secured a wager at the odds the two men were happy with. It was time. The Englishman wryly smiled and adjusted his stance. He let his half-shattered shield fall to the ground. He would only now advance, instead of retreat. Attack, not defend.

Edward drew on the memory of coming back to his village, as a boy – and finding his cottage burned to the ground and his mother and father disembowelled. The English knight would plough through the bastard in front of him, as the Normans had ploughed through his homeland. His nostrils flared, sucking in more air, stoking the fire, as hot as hell, in his chest.

His dark eyes narrowed in determination, or malice. Edward's footing was surer - and his armour no longer appeared to weigh him down - as he closed on his opponent. Victim.

The force and fury of the Englishman's assault was like nothing Girard had ever encountered during his fencing lessons. The Norman could barely retain a grip on his sword when their blades struck. Each blow upon his shield jarred his entire body. Bohemond's supporters – and anyone who had bet on Edward – cheered. Raymond's followers remained silent – and some even cringed with shame when Girard appeared to let out a small yelp in reply to the ferocity of the Englishman's attack.

When the Norman finally managed to feebly swing his sword at his opponent Edward caught the blunt blade in his gauntleted hand and yanked the weapon away, disarming his opponent. The crowd gasped once more. Wide-eyed. Astonished. But the Englishman ignored them. Instead he quickly moved forward and butted his combatant, re-shaping his fine aquiline nose.

Bone and cartilage cracked, like the snapping of a twig. Bohemond had been proved right in his judgement, when the bout had been announced:

"You may not know how to fence, but God knows you can fight, Edward."

Girard fell to the ground, with a clink and clatter. Terror spilled into the young man's heart and quivering features as the stone-faced Englishman stood over him and rested the rounded point of his sword on the Norman's blood-stained chin. There was no need to ask if he would yield. The contest was over.

"You may call yourself a nobleman, but you are no knight," Edward remarked, damningly, his voice as rough as the beard on his face.

2.

Edward sucked on each small bone from the roasted hare which had been put in front of him. He licked his fingers and made sure to finish the dregs in his cup of diluted wine. Through the entrance to the tent the vermillion sun glowed like embers on the horizon. In the background, he could hear the Orontes flow peacefully, indifferently. Come evening the jade river would appear as black as Styx.

"You earned yourself another victory this afternoon, Edward. Bohemond will duly reward you. But know also that you may have won an enemy too. I have had the misfortune to meet Raymond's nephew on more than one occasion. He is comfortably capable of base spite and revenge. He is part of the nobility after all," Adhemar de Monteil, Bishop of Le Puy, drily remarked to his friend.

Although Raymond of Toulouse and Bohemond argued that each deserved to be considered the chief military commander of the crusade, there could be no such similar debate about who was the spiritual leader of the campaign. The scene was somewhat staged, yet Adhemar's piety and purpose were sincere when he took the cross from Pope Urban II at Clermont.

The bishop was middle-aged with a kind, sage countenance, which put one at ease. His words and actions were always considered and courteous. Adhemar managed to possess both a satirical sense of humour and a sense of godliness. Edward was often impressed by the clergyman's ability to remember most the names of the people he'd meet, whether they were a prince or pauper. As well as being a gifted orator and diplomat, Adhemar was not fearful of picking up a weapon, to aid the cause. The bishop first encountered the knight when the two men found themselves fighting side-by-side at the Battle of Dorylaeum. Adhemar's leadership and bravery - when riding into the heart of the Turkish camp - turned the tide during the engagement and caused the Seljuks to rout.

"Girard will have to get in line, should he want to stab me in the back. God knows how many cuckolds, wounded Turks and wronged women are in front of him," the knight said, and then yawned.

Adhemar grinned, his aspect as bright and warm as the coals on the brazier standing in between the two men. He enjoyed the honesty and humour of the gruff Englishman, particularly when they shared a jug of wine. Edward was far from a good Christian, but the soldier was a good man. He hoped that the veteran knight could one day find some peace and contentment.

The Harrying of the North had devastated England – and the child's soul. After finding his parents dead – and village razed to the ground – Edward Kemp travelled south. One night he came across a dying campfire. The boy scavenged what food he could, before entering the service of Richard of Bolene, a Norman knight, on an estate just outside of Winchester. The baron noticed something in the strong-limbed stable hand and turned him into a squire, teaching him how to ride and fight.

"Bolene was a bawd – and I was one of his many whores, so to speak. Once I could wield a sword and lance properly, I was shipped off, with others, to fight in various campaigns across Europe, from Moorish Spain to the Italian peninsula," Edward explained to Adhemar, one evening, shortly after the Battle of Dorylaeum. "I've killed more men than I care to remember. God should, quite rightly, never forgive some of the things I've done. I've made widows and orphans of far too many people. But God turned his back on me a long time ago – and so I justly turned my back on God, to return the favour… So now I sell my sword to the highest bidder. I'm a soldier of fortune. Or rather misfortune. I would sell my soul too, if I thought it was worth anything… Why did I join Bohemond's company? He's the best of a bad bunch. And he knows how to win, whether employing might or guile. And to take Antioch, we'll need both. He puts food in our bellies and gold in our purses… There are far worse men in the world than Bohemond. And there are far worse causes to die for… But, should I somehow survive this fool's errand of a pilgrimage, I intend to return to England. Buy a farm. Get my hands dirty, instead of bloody… Thankfully the women in England like a drink, so I should be able to get some poor mare drunk enough to agree to marry me. I don't mind her being ugly, if she's a good cook. I don't mind her being poor, if she's well-endowed in other ways. And I even won't mind her being shrewish, so long as she's rich enough for me to be able to afford a more compliant mistress."

The wind blew-up and soughed through Adhemar's tent. A small wooden bed sat in the corner next to a large writing desk, inlaid with ivory. A few candles flickered below a brace of pictures, which hung above the desk. The first was an image of Christ on the cross, the second was a portrait of St Augustine. Silken tendrils of smoke spiralled upwards from sticks of incense, although the fragrance seldom eclipsed the fetid smell of ordure from the nearby latrines. Two lecterns lined the side of the tent opposite the bed. Both were in use. Partly to practise his letters – and curious to know what his friend was reading – Edward walked over to the lecterns whilst Adhemar attended to one of his clerks. The well-thumbed Bible was open at the *Book of Galatians*. The words danced before his eyes initially, but the soldier focused – squinting – and slowly took in a passage from the text. A grimy finger traced the letters over the page and his mouth opened and closed, sounding out some of the syllables.

"Only the person who is put right with God through faith shall live."

He didn't quite understand or appreciate what he was reading.

The second tome, like the first, was heavily annotated with the bishop's tiny but elegant handwriting. Again, Edward bent over the lectern and scrivener-like examined one of the annotated passages.

"Men give voice to their opinions, but they are only opinions, like so many puffs of wind that waft the soul hither and thither and make it veer and turn. The light is clouded over and the truth cannot be seen, although it is there before our eyes."

The tent was also home to a small altar. A worn purple cushion, with two indents from where the bishop knelt and prayed each morning and evening, sat on the floor, before the altar. Later that evening he prayed for God to compel Yaghi Siyan to surrender. For a divine wind to breathe life into the sails of the supply ships, coming from Cyprus. For Alexios Komnemos, the Byzantine emperor, to make haste with his army - and for Kerbogha's forces to disband or be further delayed. Should his prayers go unanswered however the bishop would not lose his faith in God (as much as his faith was wavering in his fellow man)? Adhemar would continue to work and answer his own prayers. He would support Bohemond in his undisclosed plan to capture the city (even if it meant the nobleman breaking his oath to the emperor and securing Antioch for himself). He would also oversee the distribution of supplies so that none grew fat at the expense of the starving. "A rising tide should lift all boats." He would use his agents to feed false intelligence to the enemy, such as they did when convincing Kerbogha that Baldwin's fortified town of Edessa possessed riches to rival those held at Jerusalem. Every day that Kerbogha was delayed, fruitlessly trying to capture the

RICHARD FOREMAN

stronghold, granted the pilgrims additional time to capture Antioch or be joined by the emperor's army. To concentrate Alexios' mind, Adhemar had written to his ally inferring that Bohemond intended to conquer Antioch for himself. Rather than being reinforced by a Byzantine army, he feared the campaign might lose a Frankish one soon. Stephen of Blois was wavering in his commitment to the cause. Either he was ill, or feigning illness. His words said one thing, but his eyes said another, as Adhemar tried to bolster the prince's courage.

"I will pray for you anyway, Edward, lest Girard desires to put himself first in the line to stab you in the back," Adhemar said, pouring his remaining measure of wine into his guest's cup.

"Well, God has already just answered my prayers, as I asked him for more wine. But if you must insist on praying for my wellbeing please implore the Almighty to provide me with a sturdy horse."

"I may be able to provide that myself."

"How do you know that I won't abandon you and ride off into the sunset with the mount?"

"I trust you."

"That must be the drink talking."

"Perhaps. But I believe that you have never broken your word, Edward."

"That's because I've never given it."

"You are still a good man, for a knight."

"And you're an honest man, for a priest."

"Touché. But more so let us hope Bohemond proves a good and honest commander. At our last council meeting he promised he would be able to take the city. His price, if successful, will be to take control of the Antioch. When he put forward his proposal some time ago I, like other council members - Raymond, Robert of Normandy and Godfrey –

refused to acquiesce to the idea. Our honour demanded that we return Antioch to the emperor. The avarice and pride of the other princes would not allow Bohemond to covet the city for himself either. But necessity has ground down opposition. Raymond asked me before the meeting if I could scupper Bohemond, but desperate times call for desperate measures. We have already sacrificed too many lives. So, I endorsed Bohemond's proposal. We will need to be on the other side of Antioch's walls when Kerbogha's army arrives, else prayers alone will be all that we have to deliver us," Adhemar asserted. He stared into space as he spoke and shivered a little, either from fear or the cold breeze blowing through the entrance of the tent.

"If it was anyone else but Bohemond I would put his promise to take the city down to Norman hubris. You will forgive me I hope if I don't rely on the power of prayer or God to save us. God may even be to blame for luring us into this lion's den – where we'll shortly be mauled to death. If anything, we are being punished for our sins, perhaps by the Jewish God for the massacres at Mainz and Cologne. Or by a Muslim God for the aftermath at Dorylaeum. For my part, I'll be praying for some old-fashioned good luck instead of divine intervention. In my experience, good luck is a far more consistent commodity than God's favour. But what will be will be. Or inshallah, as our enemies often spout. There are worse fates than death. For one, I could be married to an ugly, poor English shrew - who can't cook!"

3.

His legs felt like they might buckle, either from fatigue or the fear of having to explain his defeat to his uncle, Raymond of Toulouse. Girard kept his head lowered, his chin digging into his chest, as he made his way through the camp. Past rows of tents, stables, blacksmiths and campfires. Past all manner and races of men: Franks, Greeks, Armenians, Germans, and Italians.

Shame and a seething fury chequered the nobleman's thoughts.

"It was a boy against a man," one spectator had said scornfully, as the crestfallen Norman rose to his feet after the contest. Godfrey of Bouillon and Robert of Flanders had turned their backs on him. The laughter from some parts of the crowd still rung in his ears. Even the birds, cawing in the background, seemed to be mocking him. He still felt the end of the Englishman's blade on his face – like an itch he could never scratch away. The adolescent gripped the hilt of his sword, to stop his hand from trembling.

Defeat and dishonour would follow him around, like the mark of Cain. Holy water couldn't wash it off. Nor wine. Nor the blood of a vanquished Turk. Perhaps only the blood of the English knight could redeem him. He needed to face and defeat his enemy in a rematch. Or kill him in his sleep, Girard darkly mused.

The whey-faced Norman trudged on, towards Raymond's billet. A few of the young nobleman's retinue trudged on behind him - mournful, as if they were walking behind a coffin. They had no desire to disturb their lord, lest he took his humiliating defeat out on them. His mood could be as changeable as a child's.

Streaks of sweat marked his dusty, tawny countenance. Sand had annoyingly entered his boots. Girard felt it in between his toes and rubbing against his heel. The short-tempered nobleman cursed the omnipresent sand as much as Kemp, or God. It found its way into his bed, his wine and victuals. Girard missed the sensation of dewy grass beneath his feet and a vernal breeze cooling his skin. Provencal – not the Holy Land – was the true realm of milk and honey, he grievously concluded. The nobleman missed hunting, basic luxuries, good wine and the laughter and flesh of his mistresses back home. Taking the cross was a mistake. How were men celebrating the glory of God by dying in their own excrement – or being slaughtered by the enemies of Christendom?

Three guards stood either side of the gate to the farmhouse, which Raymond of Toulouse had appropriated as soon as he reached Antioch. Other mere mortals billeted themselves in tents. The six surly-faced sentinels were employed for reasons of status, rather than security - especially when one considered how it was known that Bohemond posted four soldiers outside of his own billet.

The main stone building of the property was crumbling. Timbers were cracking. Outbuildings were lurching. Weeds rather than flowers sprouted up from the sun-baked ground of the courtyard. Grey vines criss-crossed the stonework, albeit visitors were unsure whether the plants were alive or dead. A pillar of smoke vaunted up from the chimney and the smell of roasted pig filled his nostrils. Girard had been tempted to defy his lord and not answer for his defeat – but at least he might now receive a decent meal after enduring Raymond's ire.

A few of Raymond's soldiers were sat on benches in the courtyard. The sound of dice (carved from the bones of slaughtered animals – or Turks) could be heard, along with the end of a bawdy joke and a chorus of laughter.

As Girard approached the main door of the farmhouse, he was met by the figure of Tancred of Hauteville coming out. Although Tancred was an ally – and nephew – of Bohemond he had of late been spending a notable amount of time in Raymond's company. Courting him – and being courted. The dividing lines between allies and enemies were drawn in shifting sands. Tancred was keen to come out of the shadow of his uncle and establish himself as a powerful lord in his own right. At the start of the campaign Tancred had been a largely unknown and unproven knight, but none now doubted the Norman's courage and ambition.

"I do not want to go down in history as merely being my uncle's second in command," Tancred had remarked to Raymond, during their meeting.

"Adhemar advised me that, given my years, I can afford to be patient. But patience is not a virtue. It is rather a form of weakness, I warrant."

The afternoon sun shone off his bright armour. Though only a year or so older than Girard, Tancred carried himself with the stern authority of a knight twice his age. His features were hard, his heart even harder. His blade had tasted blood – and was thirsty for more. The prince had already proven himself as a successful commander, having taken the major towns of Tarsus and Adana during his passage to Antioch. But he had ultimately been outwitted, or bullied, by his fellow crusader Baldwin of Boulogne. Once his power base was strong enough Baldwin abandoned the campaign – breaking his oaths to both Urban and Alexios - to establish himself as a ruler of the region, off the back of Tancred's initial victories. Baldwin's mercenary behaviour (which had culminated in him controlling the town of Edessa, after betraying his erstwhile ally, Thoros) had further strengthened Tancred's determination to be a king in his own right – answerable to no one. Many condemned Baldwin for his lack of honour and loyalty. Tellingly, Tancred had also refused to swear an oath of loyalty to the emperor. The soldier had relinquished his rightful spoils of war to another man for the last time.

Girard moved aside to allow the stolidly built knight past. He both envied and feared the prince.

"Good day, Tancred. I hope we will be able to share some wine soon. We'll get some women in too."

"I have more important things on my mind than women and wine. And you should too, especially given your risible performance earlier, against the Englishman. Wine and women have made you weak. It is why your strength failed you," the prince replied, little disguising his contempt, as his hand rested on the ornate pommel of his sword. Tancred sneered and snorted simultaneously, before purposefully striding on and ignoring the nobleman as if he were a leper.

Girard grimaced and blanched, turning slightly to conceal his expression from his retinue. His entire body seemed to shrivel-up, as if he were a slug that had just had salt poured over it. And after the shame came the searing, splintering resentment again – directed not at Tancred but at himself and the ignoble Englishman. The cause of his dishonour.

My enemy.

Thomas Devin suffered hunger pangs, to the point where the young man walked, doubled-over, like a creaking grey-beard. The God-fearing Christian told himself that he was fasting – but really, he was starving. He told himself that the ration of bread and barley he had given away had gone to someone more deserving. But his stomach felt like it could reach out and snatch a crumb from the mouth of a baby.

Devin struggled to keep up with the attendant, who had been ordered by Bohemond to fetch the scribe and translator. Hugh of Cerisy was one of his most senior knights. Occasionally the stern-faced Norman turned around, pursed his lips and beckoned with his head for the youth to keep pace. Their master didn't like to be kept waiting. What did Bohemond want? Thomas sensed that he wasn't being summoned just to translate a letter. Was Bohemond about to give the order to attack the city? Or announce that they were retreating, back to Constantinople? Or marching on, to Jerusalem?

Thomas was keen to see Bohemond. He needed part of the money the prince was holding for him for safekeeping. His father, an affluent merchant, had only permitted his son to journey to the Holy Land if he travelled with Bohemond's company and carried sufficient funds. Oswald Devin had been a friend and moneylender to Robert Guiscard, Bohemond's father. The son was happy to receive the elderly merchant's friendship – and gold – too.

Thomas had promised to donate a portion of his wealth to Adhemar, to purchase provisions and distribute to the needy. Edward had recently chided the adolescent for his over-charitable heart. Or the cynical knight was sometimes bemused – or amused - by his gullible, or Christian, behaviour:

"You're a holy fool, lad. Given the chance, people will bleed you dry. That's what people do. And you'll soon be left with nothing, like them. They'll then forget your name quicker than a whore will forget the name of her latest customer, just as soon as she closes the door on him."

A wry grin animated the usually pensive boy's expression as he remembered how his father had called him a "holy fool" too, when he announced his intention to join the armed pilgrimage to Jerusalem. Any words of caution he heard from his mother and father however were drowned out by the voice and wisdom of Urban's sermon at Clermont, still fresh in his ears.

The council of clergy, headed by the supreme pontiff, took place in November, in south-eastern France. Such was the volume of people, numbering four hundred or more, Pope Urban II and his audience couldn't fit into the cathedral. Rather a platform was constructed outside and his papal throne placed upon it.

A sea of congregates stood before him, including archbishops, bishops and abbots. Noblemen and commoners stood together too, in reverent silence; their ears pricked to attention to hear the historic sermon. It had been decades since a Pope had blessed France with a significant sermon. The wind chilled the youth's pink complexion, but Urban's words would soon fire his heart.

Urban's face, his beard neatly trimmed, appeared devotional and determined. He partly projected authority through finery. The gold thread embroidering his fur-lined robes shone in the sunlight. His voice carried across the emerald field, as if borne on wings.

"O race of Franks, race from across the mountain, race chosen by and beloved by God... To you our discourse is addressed and for you our exhortation is intended. We wish you to know what a grievous cause has led us to your company, what peril is threatening you ... An accursed race, a race alienated from God, has invaded the lands of Christians... Altars have been destroyed and desecrated, baptismal fonts smeared with the blood of the fallen. Our fellow Christians are tortured to death. They are tied to stakes and pierced with arrows, dragged along the ground by their extremities, disembowelled, circumcised and beheaded. Women are sold into slavery and raped, children cruelly executed... Christians are being forced to pay illegal taxes and convert to nefarious religious practices... I have heard stories too of the infidel peeling back the skin of merchants, believing there to be riches beneath. The vile Turks have also been mercilessly cutting open stomachs, believing that humble pilgrims have swallowed gold or silver. We must avenge the fallen and protect the living... The barbarians are at the gates, the gates of Heaven. Our enemies have taken possession of Jerusalem and the Holy Sepulchre – the sacred ground where Christ sacrificed himself for us and died for our sins. The Holy City is in the hands of deplorable heathens. The road to Jerusalem must be made safe for pilgrims. We must regain the prize, both worldly and divine, of Christ's city – and be able to walk again in the hallowed footsteps of our Lord."

The supreme pontiff here paused in his oratory, perhaps overwhelmed by his own words. But any silence was quickly filled by a section in the crowd, which grew in strength and numbers each time the refrain was sounded out, like the clarion call of a trumpet.

"God wills it! God wills it."

Urban raised his ringed hand and commanded silence. He hadn't yet finished his speech. Far from it. Thomas stood rapt. His chest swelled with compassion, for those Christians suffering from the brutality of the Turk. Justice, vengeance, fired his innards, like bellows, too. He wrote to his father that evening about how their pope was both Cicero and St Augustine. Urban was a conduit of God, a vessel for divinity, as Christians congregated before him in the field at Clermont.

"I call upon our knights. Nobility has its responsibilities... In saving others, you will be saving your own soul. 'Twill be a just war, against an unholy foe... The church will offer a remission of sins, in return for your service. Your lands will be protected during your absence, during your mission to protect the East from further enemy incursions. The pestilence of the Turks is already occupying the borders of the Byzantine Empire. How long before they stand at the gates of Constantinople – and then Rome? For if Constantinople falls, that great province of civilisation and Christianity, the infidel's bloodlust will not be sated. They will not be content until they plunder and put Clermont and the whole of the west to the sword… We must heal the schism between our churches and unite under one banner. Rome and Constantinople serve one God… Your fellow Christians in the East are your blood-brothers, your comrades-in-arms, born of the same womb as you, for you are the sons of the same Christ and the same Church. The West must aid the East. We must turn any animus we harbour towards our neighbour and direct it towards our shared foe."

"God wills it! God wills it!"

Thomas found himself mouthing and then chanting the phrase too, as the crowd spoke with one voice. Knights placed their gloved hands on pommels - and clutched the crosses they wore around their necks. This was the first time the diligent student and devout Christian had travelled from his home. He had almost chosen to prolong his stay at the monastery at Cluny, but Thomas now felt that he had been called to Clermont. It was fate. God's will.

Urban's voice grew even stronger, surer – as did the congregation's responses. His beatific features became bellicose.

"Christ called us, "to take up the cross and follow me." I call upon you all, in the name of Christ, to take up the cross in an armed pilgrimage. We must liberate Jerusalem, expel the infidel and answer the call to arms of our Christian brothers in the East."

"God wills it! God wills it!"

Not a soul in the crowd remained mute. The thunderous sound vaunted upwards, past the spire of the cathedral, to the heavens.

21

"Let that be a war-cry for you in battle because it came from God. When you mass together to attack the enemy, this cry sent by God will be a cry of all – "God wills it! God wills it!""

Spontaneously, or seemingly so, Bishop Adhemar rose to his feet, walked towards his eminence and bent his knee. His beard and build were fuller than his superior's. His firm, noble features were softened with grace and deference. The crowd fell silent, slightly open-mouthed, as if enthralled by a piece of theatre. In a clear, resolute voice, brimming with devotion, the much-admired bishop beseeched his holiness to be able to make the journey to Jerusalem. To take up the cross.

He was the first to do so. The first of many.

4.

Thomas made his way through the camp, following at the heels of the dutiful Hugh of Cerisy, who marched briskly. The stern-looking knight was not in a mood to tarry - or allow Thomas to tarry either. Bohemond had instructed him to fetch the Englishman. Campfires were sprouting up like shrubbery. Soldiers sat around, half-drunk or bored – darning clothes, sharpening blades or staring into the distance (remembering happier times or dreading the future). Night was oozing into the sky, like someone opening-up a vein. A dark purple was fading to black. Thomas could still observe the crowd, swelling in numbers, in a clearing on the plain. Their silhouettes flitted about like ghosts. Peter the Hermit had already commenced his sermon.

"Faith that isn't tested is no faith at all… We are about to be encircled by an army of heathens. Let them come and fall on our swords, as Joshua smote the Canaanites and Michael drove out Lucifer and his acolytes from Heaven. 'Tis the foul infidel Kerbogha, not us, who is about to be ambushed. By a vengeful God!"

Thomas' expression became pinched, like he had just swallowed some sour wine, as he caught wind of the preacher's words. The son of the wool merchant thought that the demagogue lacked the nobility and intellect of Bishop Adhemar, but the peasantry was still rapt by his siren song. After Clermont, Peter had travelled across France and Germany, calling people to join his pilgrimage. He talked of visions and prophecies. He claimed the Second Coming was nigh, with devilish relish. The Apocalypse was on the horizon. People should save themselves. Or there was little they could do to save themselves. "We're all damned." Thomas sensed that Peter would rather be proved right than wrong – even if, by being proved right, hordes of people would suffer. He urged his flock to repent, not through words but deeds. He was the leader of a cult, as opposed to congregation. Thomas even heard stories of pilgrims plucking hairs out of the Hermit's donkey, as if they were holy relics. The preacher was one of the first to spread the word of Urban's sermon at Clermont. Taking the cross would expatiate sins. It would be a "People's Crusade," formed of men, women and children. The ordinary could become extraordinary. By being closer to Jerusalem, men would be closer to God and Heaven. They gave up everything, not that they had much to begin with. The low-born were attracted to him, like iron filings attracted to a magnet, Thomas judged. The preacher pulled brigands and knights into his orbit too. Many of the pilgrims perished, being slaughtered by Greeks and Turks alike, before even reaching Constantinople. Their souls may have been willing, but their bodies were too weak to fight off the enemy and endure the hardships of the terrain. Yet still the preacher could cast a spell and the shepherd still led his flock. Thomas had overheard Bohemond call the preacher "an irritant, but a necessary one… His aspect gleams with the Holy Spirit, or too much wine… With food in such short supply, let the people swallow his false hope and lies." The student had encountered the preacher on more than one occasion. The wizened "Hermit" tried to project an air of humility and piety. But his eyes were two slits. Serpentine. His mouth was as twisted as his logic. Thomas sometimes compared Adhemar to the unsavoury preacher. It was like comparing Hyperion to a satyr. Thomas recalled how his clothes were little better than rags and his breath reeked of fish or wine, or an unholy concoction of both. "I can't believe how God could favour someone so ill-dressed and so foul-smelling," Bohemond also commented. The self-proclaimed shepherd had shown his true colours recently, when he deserted the camp. Tancred rode out and tracked the caitiff down. Bohemond duly castigated the errant preacher in private, not wishing to diminish the popular figurehead in public.

Thomas walked on, sometimes trotting to keep up with the Bohemond's loyal lieutenant. Such an important messenger heralded an important message, the scribe reasoned. Night grabbed the sky by the throat even more, yet Thomas could still just about make out the walls of Antioch, looming large in the background, like a gigantic tombstone. The tombstone was blank. Was it waiting for all their names to be etched into it? It wasn't just the fall in temperature which caused a chill to slither down his spine. The scribe wasn't quite sure if he was more terrified of attacking the well-fortified town and being slaughtered in the breach – or getting caught between Kerbogha's approaching army and soon to be bloodied walls. He gulped in fear and felt his gut tighten, like a garrotte. Yet still Thomas told himself that the call of Jerusalem was stronger than that of his homeland. There was no going back. The young, devout pilgrim had taken the cross. He was not about to forsake his duty. God would protect them. Save them. He could feel the Almighty with him, as sure as he could feel the cold wind against his skin, or the bone hard ground beneath his feet. *Jerusalem*. The philosophy student never wondered if he was becoming a victim of his own strain of false hope and lies.

The silhouette of Bohemond's banner, unfurled and fluttering in the breeze, hoisted upon a spear, could also been seen in the gloom. The prince's billet was made up of an array of intersecting tents. Thomas noticed that an extra couple of guards had been posted at the entrance, although his attention was soon focussed on the potent smell of roasted meats which wafted out from the camp. It was as though Thomas' stomach turned itself into the shape of a hand and reached out to the ambrosial aroma. He would feel slightly guilty should Bohemond invite him to take part in a feast, given the condition of some of his fellow emaciated pilgrims, but Thomas would accept. Or his stomach would accept on behalf of the rest of him. He would endeavour to smuggle some food out, at the end of the evening, and distribute to the more deserving, however.

A number of knights gave the callow scribe scornful or suspicious looks as he made his way through the camp. Although they trusted and liked Edward, who had fought beside them and proved his mettle, the Normans had yet to embrace the other Englishman in Bohemond's company, who had still to draw a weapon and stand in a shield line with them.

The smell of body odour, ordure, ale and wine soon overpowered that of the suckling pig he nosed previously. The air was also littered with the sound of the odd belch, fart and cackle of laughter, in response to a ribald joke. Night gifted a tinge of threat and doom to everything. Drink could cause one of the Normans to lash out at the frightened Englishman at any moment. They often mocked him, sober or drunk. Thomas wished to be back in his own tent, reading by candlelight. Adhemar had kindly lent him his copy of *The Consolations of Philosophy*, by Boethius. He had imbibed the words each evening, like the soldiers had swallowed wine and ale.

"All fortune is good fortune; for it either rewards, disciplines, amends, or punishes, and so is either useful or just."

His heart beat faster and his features turned pale as Thomas grew closer to Bohemond. His meeting with him might prove neither useful nor just. He thought it best not to ask for his money. Something more important, or ominous, was at stake. Butterflies flapped in his belly, as if he were a suitor about to meet his intended for the first time. He had never been summoned this late to a meeting before. Thomas, prone to feeling guilt, raced through various scenarios where he might have transgressed. The Norman had always been quicker to punish than forgive. He felt nauseous. But, as he hadn't eaten, Thomas comforted himself that he wouldn't be able to actually sick-up anything in his employer's intimidating presence.

Hugh led the youth into a tent, which contained all manner of weaponry (swords, lances, and maces) and pieces of polished armour. The iron and steel had been oiled and polished, but spots of rust and blood could still be discerned if one examined the items closely. The accoutrements of war all belonged to Bohemond. None of the weapons were ceremonial or merely there for decoration. All had been employed to wound or kill over the years.

A couple of oil lamps, like giant fireflies, hung from the roof. Edward offered his fellow Englishman a reassuring nod, although it did little to quell the anxiety gnawing at his guts. His mouth was as dry as the cracked, leather belt clasped around his scrawny waist.

Hugh stood to attention next to Edward, his conical helmet under his arm. His other hand rested on the pommel of his broadsword. The faithful lieutenant, the bastard son of a Norman priest, was alert and ever ready to carry out his duty. A silver crucifix, hanging over his heart, glinted in the light. Service to God and Bohemond were all that mattered to the soldier, but not necessarily in that order.

"Thank you, Hugh," Bohemond said to his knight and friend, gratefully yet unsmilingly, as he rose to his feet. The military commander had been sitting behind a table, which was laden with various maps and pieces of correspondence. A bejewelled silver goblet of diluted wine was in easy reach on the sturdy oak table.

Thomas shifted his feet and nervously chewed the skin on the inside of his mouth. His eyes flitted between Edward, Hugh and

Bohemond – as they all stared at him. The air chilled the film of sweat forming on his brow. When he breathed out, it sounded like a sigh.

Bohemond half-smiled. Partly he wished to put the scribe more at ease. Partly his fretfulness amused him. Bohemond stood in front of the youth, towering over him. Despite all that the adolescent had witnessed and endured on their pilgrimage so far, he still retained an air of naiveté and innocence, which Bohemond found mildly intriguing. The Norman prince was also aware however that, despite his age, the scribe was twice as learned as scholars and clergy double his years. The youth had a gift for languages, was well read and, although he could become tongue-tied when he spoke, possessed an eloquent turn of phrase when expressing himself in writing. The Englishman was an asset. Bohemond had invested some time in getting to know the youth. He now hoped that his investment would pay off.

"There is no need to appear so worried," Bohemond remarked, placing a firm but fraternal hand on the youth's shoulder. "You have cause to be happy, rather than a feared. For more than any priest, Thomas, you are about to be given the opportunity to save everyone."

Save for a crown, Raymond of Toulouse appeared every inch a king, as he sat on a large lion-footed chair, on a raised platform, in the main chamber of his billet. Gold rings, studded with gems, decorated his fingers. Incense burned in the corner. The platform was flanked by braziers. A tapestry, depicting one of the Frank's victories, was mounted behind him.

With a wave of his hand the nobleman had dismissed his retinue, except for Girard and the knight, Henri of Bayeux. Raymond had deliberately kept the former waiting after his arrival earlier, while the rest of his close circle and kinsmen feasted in the adjoining chamber. No matter how much his stomach groaned, or the nearby laughter stung his ears, Girard dared not defy his uncle and leave the camp. He had already displeased the powerful prince. He did not wish to anger him further.

The count's visage was a blend of nobility and brutality. His brow was corrugated in scorn, his nostrils flared in ire. His hands gripped the arms of his chair, like talons – his knuckles as white as coral. His size, wealth and bearing projected authority. The nobleman considered himself superior, in more ways than one. The veteran commander's fame was legion – and not just because he commissioned scribes to write letters and books about his victories and achievements. Raymond had been the first knight to take up the cross and pledge himself – and his army – to the historic pilgrimage. Where Raymond led, others would follow. Such was the speed of his response that people rightly judged that Urban had forewarned the count about his sermon. Immediately Raymond demanded that, whilst his friend Adhemar be given the title of the spiritual leader of their company, Urban should grant him overall military command of the campaign. The politic pope refused, however. Urban had no desire to discourage other princes from pledging to join the cause, for fear of believing they would all be serving under the irascible Frank's banner. Urban had offered his friend the title of "First Among Equals," in order to satisfy the nobleman's pride. Although Raymond still pledged his support, he balked at the meaningless title and was far from mollified. But now he would have embraced the small mark of authority and prestige, for fear of people bestowing the title on his rival Bohemond.

Raymond received word that Bohemond had made contact with someone inside Antioch, who was willing to betray the city. A recent council meeting between the great princes of the pilgrimage agreed to consider ceding Antioch to Bohemond, should he be able to lift the siege. He hoped the decision could be overturned, however.

Girard stood before his uncle, head bowed, like a penitent awaiting a potentate's judgement. Defeating Bohemond's champion had been his chance to impress his commander, earn his trust and be rewarded. But he had failed.

Raymond's nephew was not the only person to disappoint him of late. Even his old friend, Adhemar, had sided with Bohemond. In the past few months there had been a sea-change in the campaign. People were turning to Bohemond to take command of the crusade (although, thankfully, Tancred had come out of his uncle's shadow and was willing to follow his own ambitions, rather than merely serve Bohemond's interests). Raymond's authority had been eroded. To his shame, even some of his men deserted him. He vowed to turn back the tide and reassert his position. Like Caesar, the nobleman would rather be the first man in a village than the second man in Rome. Or Antioch. Or Jerusalem. He had right on his side, in thwarting Bohemond. The princes had given their word in Constantinople to give the city to the Emperor, rather than claim it as their own. Raymond needed to wrestle control back from Bohemond for the good of all the pilgrims. The upstart would not be able to lead the Armies of God to victory over Kerbogha. "I am a proven leader, rather than mere pretender. We have travelled too far, sacrificed too much, to surrender now. And surrender will mean death. The Turks will slaughter us like sheep, if we allow Bohemond to lead our forces," Raymond had argued to Adhemar, but to little avail.

It was time to take matters into his own hands, the veteran determined. He had received intelligence, from Tancred, that Hugh of Cerisy, along with the English knight Edward Kemp, were due to meet with a confederate of the Antiochene insider tomorrow night. The plan to take the city would be discussed. Hopefully he would be able to steal the plan - and utilise the information himself. If the Antiochene was willing to betray his city, he would doubtless be willing to betray Bohemond too.

"I have received more than one report back about the contest. I am ashamed of you. You should be far more ashamed of yourself, of course," Raymond proclaimed, sourly, as if he had just eaten an overly brackish olive. His voice was clear, deep – as hard and unyielding as iron. There was a slight rasp to his speech, however, like the scratching sound of a rusty blade being pulled out of a warped scabbard.

Girard took an intake of breath and was about to explain himself, but his uncle quietened him by raising the palm of his hand.

"I do not wish to hear paltry excuses. You were not unlucky. Rather you were lucky that the Englishman didn't cause you serious injury. You are also fortunate now, that I do not thrash you like an errant child. Instead, I am going to offer you an opportunity to regain your honour. If you bear any resemblance to a Christian knight you will endeavour to redeem yourself. You suffered from the sin of pride," Raymond declared, without irony. "You promised your men the fruits of victory. I suggest you compensate them out of your own purse. You told me that you possessed the skill and mettle to defeat the Englishman. God's blood, an Englishman! He was probably half-drunk."

Raymond seethed, rather than breathed. He in part blamed himself. His nephew's fencing teacher, back in France, had praised his student. He wanted to add to his family's prestige, by championing his kinsman. Bohemond had defeated him, by proxy. The injury to his pride would smart, fester, for some time. The nobleman had also underestimated the lowly Englishman. He would not make the same mistake twice. Nor would he publicly admit any blame. Girard needed to feel culpable – and desire to atone for his shame.

Finally, his nephew - and his small company of men - would be of some use, Raymond considered. He would charge Girard with following Hugh and the Englishman. Tancred mentioned that Bohemond would order the two knights to rendezvous with the contact. Should Girard fail, and be apprehended, Raymond could employ the excuse that he had attacked the Englishman out of revenge for his recent, ignominious defeat. To ensure the mission proved successful he would task Henri with leading Girard's men.

The nobleman glanced at his lieutenant, who was staring at his nephew with thinly veiled contempt. The sneer on his face was even more pronounced than usual. Henri had nicknamed Girard "the whelp". The knight was tempted to challenge Kemp to a contest, to regain his prince's honour, but he preferred to stay in the shadows. The mercenary had killed plenty of men, English or otherwise, during his career. He had nothing to prove – and any fight which wasn't a fight to the death was a mere mime show.

Henri, who was approaching his fortieth year, was dressed in a black, leather jerkin and dark brown leather trousers. His muscular build could be discerned beneath the cut of his clothes. The Norman had a narrow, coffin-shaped head. Swollen, radish coloured gums housed a set of sharp yellow teeth. Dark, deep set eyes sat over a long, blade-like nose. His hawkish expression took in everything – and glowered at Girard as if he were imagining how he might murder him.

Henri was the second son of a Norman soldier. He learned his trade as a man-at-arms and a sword for hire – serving in Spain, England and Italy. He was an accomplished swordsman, equestrian and archer. Raymond immediately recognised the mercenary's talents and employed him as a knight in his company (who could also serve as an assassin and spy). The soldier put a high price on his services, but the expense was worth it.

A chill ran down his spine as Girard felt the knight's cold glare upon him. Two rumours assaulted his thoughts. The first was that the mercenary kept two poisonous snakes, Adam and Eve, as pets – partly because he used the venom to bait the blades of his weapons. The second was that Henri had slit the throat of his own bastard son, when he caught him embezzling funds. If he could kill a fourteen-year-old boy, his own kin, then the soldier was capable of killing anyone, Girard reasoned.

"I am going to grant you an opportunity to regain your honour - and damn the Englishman in the process," Raymond added, picking a piece of pork out from between his teeth. "You will submit yourself and your company to the authority of Henri and follow his every order."

Girard nodded, with deference and enthusiasm – a confection of fear and vengeance. He felt light-headed – and not just because he was famished.

The knight's expression remained unmoved. Implacable. Should he cross swords with Hugh or Kemp tomorrow evening, then so be it. Whatever it took to complete the mission. Part of him wanted to test himself against the famed combatants. Should the whelp perish in any engagement, then so be it too.

If God wills it…

Bohemond. He could be as ferocious as a barbarian, or as charming as a diplomat, Thomas thought. His father was Robert Guiscard, the Norman conqueror. Robert the Wily. His son could be considered even wilier though. Like his father, Bohemond had employed military might, as well as political guile, to take control of huge swathes of the Italian peninsula. The Norman had spent half his life at war, whether battling his own brother or the might of the Byzantine Empire. Thomas had even heard a rumour circulate that Bohemond had compelled Pope Urban to call for his armed pilgrimage in order to secure a foothold in Greek and Turkish territories. "He's as ambitious as Caesar," Adhemar once remarked, his voice laced with anxiety rather than admiration. The bishop had seen Bohemond's courage and martial prowess at first hand - and was grateful for having the Norman as an ally, instead of an enemy. The prince had displayed personal bravery and military genius on more than one occasion throughout the campaign.

Constant campaigning meant that Bohemond was well conditioned. His brawny arms and broad chest made him resemble an archer. His waist was narrow, but not due to starvation. His skin was as smooth as marble, or his tongue. His short, light brown hair had grown fair in the sun. Bohemond had been clean shaven when he set out for Constantinople, all those months ago, but a neatly trimmed beard now lined his lantern jaw. Despite having disfigured many an enemy on the battlefield, Bohemond had remained unmarked. Handsome. His blue eyes could appear piercing, bright or cold – depending on the prince's mood. His demeanour oozed confidence, or arrogance. He owned an air of knowing more than anyone else in the room - and knowing more than he was willing to impart. Unlike other princes, Bohemond seemed un-tempted by the sins of the flesh. As much as he might utilise high-risk strategies on the battlefield, Bohemond had no interest in gambling or other pastimes of his fellow noblemen. Instead, the Norman prince lusted after power – and he was content to wade knee-deep, or even waist-deep in blood, to reach its shores.

"I have recently been in contact with an armourer, inside the city. His name is Firuz. Although an Armenian, he became a Muslim convert after settling in Antioch. It seems he is as capricious as a woman in his loyalties, but that is to our benefit.

Firuz has been charged with guarding part of the city walls, close to the Gate of St George. He first made contact through passing a message to Tancred's forces there. His initial inspiration, behind betraying his city, was that God compelled him to act. He claims to have received three visions from Christ, no less. I have faith in my doubts that the condition of his soul is not Firuz's only motivation. If Christ has promised him heaven, I have promised him the earth, however, to help break the siege. I have received intelligence reports confirming his grievance against Yaghi Siyan. The governor has appropriated part of the Armenian's wealth and he's understandably not best pleased. I have faith in his greed and desire for revenge, rather than in his inclination to answer any divine calling. We still need to finalise the plans for Firuz to grant us access to the city. I will need you to meet with his kinsman, one Varhan, tomorrow night. I trust you are fluent in his language, Thomas? Edward and Hugh will accompany you. A price has already been agreed, for Firuz's services. But if the treacherous cur tries to re-negotiate the deal then refer yourself to Hugh," Bohemond remarked, no stranger to treachery.

He had first opened a dialogue with Firuz, through an agent who could pass in and out of the city, some weeks ago. Bohemond was willing to play a dangerous game and wait to accept the Armenian's proposal. He would only take Antioch, if he could possess the city afterwards. At first the other princes refused his offer. They also saw through his threat to abandon the pilgrimage, in order to attend to the discord in his homeland. But Bohemond was prepared to wait, until his brothers-in-arms were desperate and doomed. He knew that his fellow noblemen didn't much like him, but they would swallow their pride and enmity because they needed him. Kerbogha was coming, with an army that could grind them into dust. To survive, the pilgrims needed to be inside Antioch's walls, as opposed to being locked out of them. Exposed. They would be target practise for hordes of Turkish archers, with the scent of blood in their nostrils. Some of the princes suspected Bohemond of behaving dishonourably, but they could only furnish people with rumour instead of proof. Even if he was of the devil's party, the Norman was the only saviour they had. The council finally agreed to his terms. In return, Bohemond would answer their prayers. For those who protested that he was breaking his oath to the Emperor, the Norman asserted that Alexios broke his oath first, by abandoning the pilgrims. They had more chance of seeing a dragon, or washing the blackamoor white, than having Alexios and a Greek army join their cause. Their vow, contract, was annulled, Bohemond argued.

"Tis as if we were man and wife, but the marriage was never consummated."

Bohemond pictured Alexios – the arch-treacherous bastard - now. The womanish Greek was draped in silk, dripping in gold, doused in perfume and spouting pious, obsequious phrases. He was fond of making war – by getting others to fight his battles for him. He wanted to be the emperor of the world, but he couldn't even keep his own people safe. The empire was crumbling under his leadership. Alexios had taken his begging cup to Urban, mewling like a child. He didn't deserve to rule Antioch, Bohemond judged. The Norman would not spill his own blood, and the blood of his men, in order to hand the city over to a coward and his court of whores and eunuchs. To the victor must go the spoils. Bohemond knew that Adhemar was not happy with his actions. He liked and respected the bishop, who knew how to wield a sword, as well as his pen. "But I was put on this world to make myself happy. Not Adhemar. Or Urban. Or Raymond of Toulouse. Or Alexios."

The prince had originally bowed his head to the Emperor, in order to keep his eyes on the prize. The two former adversaries realised they needed each other. Mutual cooperation overruled mutual distrust. The Emperor needed Bohemond's leadership and army. Bohemond needed the Emperor's provisions and supply chain. But the two leaders also realised that they would eventually betray one another. It was just a matter of which one of them would betray the other first.

Thomas gulped and nodded his head in assent, torn between hope and dread. He would do his duty, like the chivalrous knights he had read about in the *Song of Roland* and chronicles of Charlemagne. He was resolved to venture to the village, to meet with Bohemond's contact and attempt to save the crusade. Or he would die trying.

5.

A small lamp in the corner illuminated Edward's tent. The light reflected off the film of perspiration on the woman's breast. Both Edward and Emma were still a little breathless, after making love. The madam, who oversaw a number of whores linked to Bohemond's camp, now spent most of her evenings with the English knight. Strands of black hair stuck to her forehead and cheeks. Occasionally he caught the sound of her bracelets and anklets clinking together. Edward promised himself that he would one day buy her a piece of jewellery, to remember him by, when the opportunity arose. If the opportunity arose. She rested her head on his scar-littered chest. Emma once asked about his wounds. But the soldier just shrugged his shoulders in reply.

"I could offer you some tales of valour and chivalry. But I can't rightly remember if the scars are from battles, tavern brawls or ex-lovers. Women know the weaknesses in a man's armour, far more than any Turk."

Her olive complexion had bronzed in the summer sun. Her green eyes could often flash like Greek fire, if her temper was provoked. But at other times her aspect could prove uncommonly kind – and kindness was in short supply in and around Antioch, Edward judged. Her face was lean, hard – but a fading beauty could still be a beauty. Emma was past her prime, but who wasn't? Experience owned plenty of advantages and virtues over youth too.

Edward had seen Emma in the camp several times – and had spent the evening with an array of her girls – but he spoke to the madam in earnest a few months ago, at a feast to celebrate a victory over a Turkish army, led by Bohemond. He looked her up and down, appraising her figure as if he were about to purchase a horse. Emma scrutinised the knight, assessing how wealthy the pilgrim might or might not be.

"I've never been with an Englishman before," the veteran prostitute remarked, smiling and narrowing her almond eyes, as if purring. She was wearing a red, linen dress with a low neckline. Her black tresses were artfully pinned-up, showing off her elegant shoulders and neck.

"You are about to experience one of the biggest anti-climaxes of your life then," Edward grinningly replied, pouring the woman a cup of wine. "We English are such renowned drunkards. We couldn't possibly be renowned lovers too. My money will be good though, even if my performance in bed won't be. Unlike other knights, I'll try not to tell you the story of my life and bore you to sleep."

Emma laughed – and laughter was in short supply in and around Antioch.

Bohemond had invited the madam (who owned a brothel in Taranto) and her girls to join his company on their pilgrimage. His men would need entertaining during the campaign. The prostitutes would have a captive audience.

"Just make sure that none of your whores are pox-ridden," the prince warned – although he couldn't give a similar assurance for his own men. "You will be a wealthy woman when you return."

Emma had at first declined the nobleman's offer. But Bohemond was not accustomed to hearing the word no. He threatened to bow to pressure from a local priest to close the brothel or raise the taxes on the establishment. And so Emma and her girls joined the pilgrimage. Business was good. She had indeed become a wealthy woman. But what good would come of it, if she wouldn't be able to return home? Emma had thought about abandoning the pilgrimage on more than one occasion, but the road west would prove even more perilous than remaining if she travelled alone.

Perhaps Edward could encourage other knights to escort her – and her girls – back to Taranto, Emma considered. Although that was not why she was with him. After their first night together, she had provided him with a discount – and then hadn't charged him at all.

"It must be love," Emma had half-joked to one of her whores, Herleva, the other day.

The lamp began to flicker. Edward ran his fingertips along the woman's back and squeezed her rump. They had barely shared a word with one another earlier, after he returned from his meeting with Bohemond, before making love. The knight wanted to drink kisses from her lips and feel the warmth of her body next to his. To find and lose himself with her.

"Did you have a good night?" Edward asked.

"It was good, as in mildly profitable. Although people are understandably spending more money to cover the rising price of food. Even noblemen are pleading poverty. I also had to work. I had one regular who wept unashamedly, crying out for his mother. He told me the story of his life, unfortunately. I had to keep pricking myself with a pin, to stay awake. How was your day?"

Edward forced a smile. He felt uncomfortable of late, imagining Emma sleeping with other men. Even though he believed her, when she said it was a matter of business rather than pleasure. Needs must. He told himself that he wasn't jealous, but that he was worried that he might catch the pox from her, should she sleep with the wrong client. Edward hadn't survived countless encounters with bloodthirsty, scimitar-wielding Turks in order to die of a pox.

"I've had worse days. I taught a lesson to some arrogant Norman peacock – and even got paid for the pleasure," the

Englishman said, declining to mention his summons and mission relating to Bohemond. Not only did he not want to earn Bohemond's wrath by disclosing his plans, but more so he didn't want to offer Emma too much hope that all would be well. Hope was worse than despair, Edward gloomily concluded. "I bought you a consignment of wine to share with the girls."

"You don't have to buy me anything."

"I know I don't have to. But I want to."

Edward refrained from saying that it was better to spend his money now, while he could. He wouldn't be able to enjoy his gold when dead.

Before having disembarked, to journey east, Adhemar had been called handsome and noble. He didn't particularly feel handsome and noble right now, however. His robes were stained and frayed. His skin felt dry, cracked, like overused parchment. His heart felt heavy, as if he were wearing an orb around his neck. During his youth a friend had predicted that Adhemar, born into a wealthy aristocratic family, would become a philosopher. He knew how to win an argument, whether employing a blade or oratory. Utilising both his good looks and charm he could have juggled more mistresses than a poet. But instead Adhemar became wedded to God. The Church provided him with a home. The Bible was all the poetry he needed. God provided him with cast-iron purpose and meaning.

Adhemar worked late into the night, partly because he knew he wouldn't be able to sleep. He finished off a letter to his friend and fellow bishop, William of Falaise, who was a trusted confidante. Increasingly, as Adhemar disclosed his sins and doubts, William was serving as his friend's confessor.

"I still believe that our cause is a noble one, despite witnessing a litany of ignoble acts. This is still a just war. As

Aristotle argued, "War must be for the sake of peace." Having observed the viciousness of the Turk, we must, now more than ever, aid our Christian brothers in the East and fight to keep their borders safe. Jerusalem must not be desecrated. The road to the Holy Land must be secured for pilgrims. For some time I believed that we could fulfil our mission. We showed unity and purpose at Nicaea. Princes came to each other's aid in battle. We have strayed from our path, however. Perhaps Raymond was right, when he argued for an all-out assault on Antioch as soon as we arrived... My faith remains strong, but it isn't strong enough for everyone. Desertions are increasing, we are losing men like water passing through a sieve. I have heard that some of the pilgrims are so desperate for nourishment that they have descended to eating boiled thistles, or the seeds of grain found in manure. As I walk through the camp each day I am approached by princes and paupers alike. They ask for my blessing and for me to pray for them. To my shame, I often forget their names. God's representatives on earth are all too human too, as you know... I spoke to a young Englishman in our ranks, the other month. Thomas. He is a gifted linguist and scholar. In another life he could have copied, or created, great works of literature. He could have been a leader in his village, served his church.

"I was there at Clermont. I am here because of you," he proclaimed, zealously and without rancour.

How much blood do I have on my hands? I scoured the land, preaching. Recruiting. I promised that sins would be forgiven, that pilgrims would find salvation. I also hinted at riches and rewards. My purpose was to inspire knights and soldiers. Urban and I never envisaged so many women and children joining our campaign... Peter the Hermit and his flock could soon be lambs to the slaughter. We will soon be caught between Kerbogha's vast army and Yaghi Siyan's garrison, five thousand strong, in

Antioch. We will be caught in a vice, butchered. Muslims do not have a Christian bone in their bodies. Those who are not tortured and killed will be enslaved. They would be spoils of war… People still say that they believe in me. But I'm not sure how much I believe in myself."

Adhemar diluted his wine. He wanted to keep a clear head and make the vintage last longer. After reading over his letter the bishop was tempted to spend the evening writing his will, but he drew himself back, like a hand withdrawing from a flame, believing that by doing so he would be admitting defeat.

The careworn clergyman emitted a mournful sigh and wanted to bury his head in his hands, but he was worried that an attendant might enter and see him in despair. He needed to be strong, or at the very least appear strong. He rose to his feet but soon fell to his knees and commenced his nightly prayers.

He prayed for Tatikios, the Byzantine general who had accompanied the pilgrimage since Constantinople. Despite deserting the campaign, under the excuse of departing to send for reinforcements, Adhemar asked God to keep Tatikios safe. He liked the clever, urbane general. The glint in his eye had matched the glint of the golden plate which covered his mutilated nose. The Emperor had attached his envoy to the pilgrimage to provide assistance to his allies, although it was also clear Tatikios was a spy – whose mission was to ensure that Antioch was delivered up to Alexios. Bohemond openly accused the Greek of treachery and even threatened his life, realising the threat he posed to his own ambitions.

Adhemar missed his company. They would discuss literature and theology, over a jug of wine, late into the night. He missed his subtle wit. With just one jibe or barb the agent could send the likes of Raymond and Baldwin into a fit of rage. The Byzantine was a shrewd judge of people. Adhemar recalled his candid character assessment, or assassination, of Bohemond.

43

"He is the worst of a bad bunch. Or somehow the best too. He is as unscrupulous as a lawyer, as untrustworthy as a priest and as barbaric as the most chivalrous knight."

The princes would be loath to admit it, but Tatikios' intelligence and tactical advice concerning their enemies had proved invaluable.

Adhemar was conscious of praying for his old friend, as well as his recent companion. He had conferred with Raymond of Toulouse, even before Clermont. Without Raymond's army their pilgrimage would have perished. Raymond had spearheaded the crusade. Before Constantinople, the Frank was one of the most powerful men in Christendom. But his beard was now more streaked with grey than brown. His hand sometimes trembled when he lifted his wine cup or sword. Raymond had told his friend that this would be his last campaign. "We will be the twin pillars of the crusade, secular and spiritual. The sword and the cross. I will answer Urban's call, for the glory of God," Raymond declared. He would die in the East, if God willed it, he confessed to Adhemar. The bishop prayed to God for an alternative fate for his companion. *Let him live. Let him see Jerusalem. Let him find peace.*

Yet the bishop wondered whether Raymond could ever find peace through arms, or in his heart. He had grown embittered – or more embittered – since the beginning of the campaign. The sin of pride ran bone deep. Pride blinded him. He would rather see Bohemond defeated, than have his rival triumph over their real enemies. Adhemar recalled the words of Tatikios:

"Raymond is a man who knows that his best years are behind him. But for all of his valour on the battlefield he lacks the courage to confront this simple truth."

Adhemar remembered how he used to host Raymond at his residence. They would talk about church reform, gossip about the affairs of local noblemen and discuss the troubles in the

East. The bishop felt a pang of regret as he pictured them both around his dinner table, sharing a fine meal in front of the hearth. He told himself that they were worldly trappings – but he longed for his library, cook, soft bed and garden. But home was, like the past, another country. One that he would never see again, he lamented.

The bishop prayed that Kerbogha and his army might somehow be delayed, that the pilgrimage could receive a stay of execution. Adhemar had been able to intervene by feeding Kerbogha false intelligence, that Edessa contained untold riches. The Turks subsequently delayed their march on Antioch, by besieging Baldwin's city. Edessa stood firm, and eventually Kerbogha turned his attention to his principle aim – of destroying the crusader army. Adhemar now prayed for some divine intervention. They would need to snatch victory, from the jaws of defeat, one last time.

At one moment the bishop seemed serene, meditating like a peripatetic philosopher, but at others he appeared in utter turmoil. His mouth twitched and his eyeballs rolled beneath his lids, like he was experiencing a nightmare. His knees creaked and ached, from too much praying.

Yet the ardent and admirable Christian continued to pray. For Bohemond. Tatikios had commented that he was "the best and worst of the Norman princes… He is as trustworthy as a Turk." Bohemond had tricked and bullied his companions into getting his own way. Yet, should he secure Antioch, all would be forgiven. He would be their Achilles and Odysseus.

A gust of wind slapped against the side of the canvas tent. One of the oil lamps burned out, plunging the bishop's altar into darkness. Before Adhemar retired though he spared one last thought and prayer for his English friend. That Edward would learn how to pray too.

6.

Morning.

Shafts of sunlight speared through clumps of cloud. The oppressive heat sapped what little strength people could muster.

The three men – Edward, Owen and Thomas – stood in a small clearing in Bohemond's camp. A few spots of blood and broken rings, which had fallen off pieces of mail during practise bouts between soldiers, littered the hard ground.

The Welshman, who would have confessed that he was far from the greatest swordsman in Christendom, rolled his eyes in exasperation as he glanced at Edward and passed judgement on Thomas' swordsmanship. He felt like running a finger across his throat, to communicate that Thomas would be a dead man, should he have to fight for his life in battle. The lesson was not going well. Despite all his previous tutelage, the scribe was still limp-wristed and flat-footed. Owen liked the lad, but he could not help him if he was unwilling to help himself. The archer had a flat, ruddy face. He enjoyed a good drink and a good bout of singing, in that order, although it had been some time since he felt that there was anything to sing about – including Thomas' progress handling a sword. The attacking and defensive moves the Welshman attempted to impart were only basic, but they still seemed beyond the student. Thomas' risible performance would have been funny, if his life wasn't at stake. He was lacking in effort and application. Time was growing short. Thomas would be called upon to fight if, or when, Kerbogha gave battle. He's a dead man walking, the bowman thought to himself.

As Owen went to retrieve his wineskin to quench his thirst Edward stepped in to have a word with Thomas. The slight, young Englishman was bent over, in a stoop, as he stood dressed in a mail shirt, his breathing laboured. His face was pinched in worry, beneath a pool of sweat. Not so much from his lacklustre display, but from the blister forming on his palm. He needed his hands free from injury, so he could write.

Edward realised that, instead of trying to offer words of encouragement to the student, he should instil fear in him. It was for the scribe's own good. The knight didn't want his fellow Englishman's blood on his hands.

"You'll soon have to enter the lion's den. But you're no fucking Daniel. You'll need more than just the power of prayer when a Turk crosses your path, wielding a gruesome scimitar. He'll happily gut you like a fish and spit on your corpse. If you think I'm saying this to put the fear of God in you, you'd be right."

"I don't think I'll ever be strong enough to handle a sword well," Thomas said, meekly, by way of an explanation. He didn't specify whether he meant he wasn't physically or mentally strong enough. Perhaps he meant both. But Edward wasn't going to allow his young friend to resign himself to defeat so easily.

"You shouldn't worry because you're not overtly strong. If you're smart – and I know that you can be smart, lad – you can cut down an enemy twice your size. You just need to target his weaknesses – and the softer targets are the best targets. As I've instructed you in the past, aim for the neck and groin. The point beats the edge."

"The point beats the edge," Thomas echoed, nodding to convey that the words were sinking in. But Edward still felt like he was pissing in the wind.

"If you don't learn how to kill a man, he'll kill you. He'll skewer you, without hesitation. If you think this heat is unforgiving, I can assure you that the Turk is less forgiving."

"To kill is a sin," the Christian replied, innocently yet assertively. Edward thought that he had finally unlocked the reason as to why the student wasn't giving his all. Or even half his all. The knight offered up his own exasperated expression and felt like saying, "God, give me strength."

"Killing will be your salvation. How many good deeds will you be able to enact when you're dead? When the choice comes down to whether you or some rotten Seljuk bastard should die, I'd prefer that you live. If God won't allow you to kill, do you think God will permit you to still wound?" Edward argued, sarcastically. "At the moment you are about as useful in a fight as a eunuch in a brothel. An elder could defeat you, with just his walking stick. Or a ten-year-old girl could out fence you with her hairbrush. Professional soldiers will not be able to carry the day alone. Pilgrims need to be armed with more than just bibles and crosses. Lambs need to become lions, else we will all be slaughtered. You bleat that thou shalt not kill. Don't be such a damned holy fool, Thomas. Even Adhemar knows when to draw his sword. There's no hiding place on a battlefield," the knight posited, although he had known plenty to bury themselves beneath corpses, surrender or run away. "Holy war is still war. Barbaric and bloody."

Thomas' face reddened, but more in anger than embarrassment.

"I don't like it when you mock God, Edward. Without God in his life, a man is nothing. An empty vessel. If God is dead, then all is permitted. Without God, we would be little more than beasts. We do not need Circe to cast a spell on us to turn us into brutes. We are prone to wander around, lost, in the dark. But the light shines in the darkness. The enemy of God isn't the devil. It's ourselves. But everyone possesses a divine spark," the Christian argued. The knight loomed over him. At any moment it appeared as if Edward might swat the youth, like an insect. But Thomas stood his ground and remained undaunted.

"I fear I doused out my divine spark some years ago, through all the wine I drank," Edward countered.

"You do not believe in a higher power, do you?"

"If God is a higher power, perhaps he should try harder. Or not try at all. If God is responsible for the world, he has a lot to answer for, regardless of our fate or not. Given the state of the world under his aegis, God may want to move aside and give someone else a chance, as Raymond needs to move aside and let Bohemond break the siege and lead our armies."

Edward was momentarily distracted as he heard Owen let out a yawn in the background, as he lay on the ground and squeezed out the last drops of liquid from his wineskin. Thomas was too focussed on wanting to win his argument, or save his friend, to pay attention to the archer.

"Man cannot fathom the full force of God's power and intentions. We must trust in God's love and intelligence. God embodies peace and harmony."

Edward scoffed, raised his hands and kicked the ground. Aghast. Bewildered.

"I am sure God is intelligent enough to appreciate the irony, to talk of peace and harmony in the shadow of Antioch, which will soon doubtless see one of the bloodiest battles in history. The world I know Thomas is not one of amity, interspersed with conflict, but it's one of war, interspersed with short periods of peace. I would question the wisdom of your God too, given his choice of Peter the Hermit to act as one of his representatives."

Thomas shook his head, either feeling sorry for his blasphemous friend or refusing to countenance his arguments.

"I will not be able to prove the existence of God for you Edward. Ultimately you will need to make a leap of faith. Faith is to believe in what you cannot see. God calls to us, but individually. Faith isn't what will damn us. It will be what delivers us. You must have heard a calling, for you to have joined the pilgrimage."

"I heard the promise of a chinking purse. You may think that everyone is here to help protect their Christian brothers. But some are here for conquest. This crusade is not act of charity, but larceny. You once said that Jerusalem represents the divine to you. For me, it represents retirement."

"I urge you to pray, Edward. Talk to God and your better self," Thomas pleaded, consciously or not clutching the cross around his neck.

"What good will it do?"

"What harm could it do? God will hear you. He is omnipresent."

"Ha! He has a perverse way of showing it," Edward replied, thinking how God was far from present during the night when his parents were slaughtered. God hadn't dared to show his face since either, the soldier considered.

"If you will not pray for yourself, I will pray for you."

"I'm happy for you to do so. God is much more likely to listen to you than me, I imagine. If you could petition the Almighty to provide me with a decent horse, who won't buckle under the weight of me while in armour. Or you could always ask God to supply me with one of his angels to bear me on his wings and carry me back to England. I would be grateful if I could be left in a spacious cottage, close to a secluded village with a tavern and a stream, plentiful with trout. Hopefully my new home will be far away from any sodomising clergymen and rapacious tax collectors. If God can furnish me with such things then I'll offer up a prayer as a thank you," Edward exclaimed, resigned to the scenario that it was unlikely he would see either England or Jerusalem.

"You shouldn't joke about God," Thomas protested, his hands balled into fists by his side. Riled. He now appeared as if he might strike the knight.

Edward couldn't help but let out a burst of withering laughter in reply. *What bigger joke was there than God?* In the background, if they chose to hear it, the Englishmen could have heard Owen snoring.

"Just take a handful of trusted men," Bohemond instructed Hugh of Cerisy. The two old friends and campaigners walked through the prince's armoury. Every now and then Bohemond would pick up a blade and scrutinise its sharpness and straightness. "If you leave the camp with too great a force you may draw attention to yourself. I would be keeping a close watch on me at the moment, so I fail to see why others wouldn't. We are so near, yet still so far, from our goal. Should it come to it, I am willing to pay more for what Firuz is offering, although hopefully he doesn't know this. Should it come to it, you will need to try and out-haggle the Armenian. But ultimately you must surrender to his terms."

The knight replied with a short nod. Bohemond trusted Hugh, as much as he could trust anyone. The two men had spilled blood on the same battlefields. The soldier had never balked at an order or sheathed his sword when his commander asked him to draw it.

As well as his service, Hugh owed Bohemond his life. During the Battle of Dorylaeum the knight was unseated from his horse. He fell to the ground. Disorientated and winded. The knight felt the tamp of hooves on the ground and gazed up to see a brace of Turkish horsemen riding towards him, their scimitars glinting in the afternoon sun. His armour seemed twice as heavy as normal. He only managed to get to his knees. His fingertips scurried across the earth, like a spider, trying to reach for his weapon. The soldier felt half-drunk, still reeling from the fall. Hugh's life flashed before him, inspiring a stinging sense of regret and failure. He rued not taking a wife and having children. He had yet to achieve any fame, so his name wouldn't live on. He would die, only ever having half lived. Hugh didn't attempt to rise to his feet or form a plan to avoid the imminent attack. He would surrender to death, rather than to the enemy. The knight prayed, quickly and potently, like a couple of sword thrusts, for God to forgive his sins and for the pilgrims to liberate Jerusalem. Hugh closed his eyes, believing he would never open them. But a killing blow never came, or at least the Norman didn't suffer a killing blow. Bohemond, his nostrils flared as much as his snorting destrier, charged into the first Turk. Flank slammed against flank. Bohemond's blade, already slick with the blood of his enemies, pierced through the Seljuk horseman's ribs, as he found a gap in the Muslim's armour. The second Turk, his face twisted in rage at the death of his kinsman, carried a large shield, which rendered him invulnerable to the Christian's sword. But the enemy's horse was unarmoured. Bohemond spurred his chestnut destrier on and jabbed the point of his sword into the eye of the adjacent mount. The creature let out a piteous cry and then threw its rider.

Bohemond merely nodded at his knight, who found the strength to get to his feet. The prince then rode off, in search of his next combatant – willing to act as a keystone to bolster any weak spot in the fighting. There was a battle to be won.

To take Antioch, however, Bohemond would have to employ guile, before he could deploy his military might.

"In terms of providing some additional insurance, I have requested that Firuz smuggle his son out of the city so we can hold him as a hostage. There is still a small chance that he could play both sides. Again, I would be tempted to act treacherously. We also cannot know for certain if the Armenian isn't an enemy agent, planted by Siyan. Or it would not be beyond Tatikios to betray us. He once served in an opposing army to my father. "Janus is less two-faced than a Byzantine," my father used to say. Deceit is a badge of honour, a code, for Tatikios. I just regret not being the foe who mutilated his nose - or turned him into a eunuch. Adhemar preaches that we are one church, that I should have considered Tatikios a brother. But I was right to cast him out of our campaign. I am but following Christian teaching. Do unto others as they would do unto you," Bohemond exclaimed, baring his teeth in either a sneer or snarl.

"We do not have any choice but to put our faith in Firuz, it seems," Hugh said, thinking how he would choose his fastest mount later, lest he be riding into an ambush.

"I have faith in man's capacity for faithlessness and greed," Bohemond said, confident that the Armenian traitor would keep his word. "Hopefully his resentment towards Siyan is as substantial as his love of gold too."

The Norman prince clapped and rubbed his hands together. He permitted himself a smirk, picturing the look on Raymond's face when he saved the crusade. His aspect duly glinted, like a newly minted coin, when Bohemond imagined opening the doors to the city's treasury.

"Firuz is not the only Antiochene who has succumbed to a sense of greed," Hugh remarked, picking up a mace on a nearby table, assessing its weight and balance. "A merchant from the city has provided us with the plans to the citadel. The drawings he has given us will help with our assault, when the time comes. Would you like to view them now?"

"One step at a time, my friend. I do not want to put the cart before the horse, as much as I am looking forward to hoisting my banner over the city. As Caesar said, it is where one is positioned at the end of the race which matters. It's now, or

53

never. I remember Steven of Blois once lecturing me that Antioch was almost impregnable."

Almost.

Edward poured out a measure of ale for himself and Emma, as they sat around a murmuring campfire. They had just finished eating a bowl of pottage. Should he have been served-up the meal in a tavern, back in England, he would have condemned the dish as being akin to swill. Yet he greedily wolfed down the portion he was served. If not for Emma being present, he probably would have licked the bowl, like a dog.

"And I thought I had claim to being the most stubborn Englishman in the camp," Edward complained, still smarting from the argument with Thomas earlier. "That lad won't be the death of me, but I'm worried that he'll be the death of himself. God's blood, I swear I felt like picking him up and shaking some sense into him this morning - or shaking the damned conceit and nonsense out of him, as if I were exorcising a demon."

"I hope that you didn't have too serious a falling out. You perfidious English need to stick together, now more than ever. You know how no one likes you. Aside from, perhaps, me," Emma said, amused slightly by his irascible mood. Usually he was indifferent to what people thought of him – and Edward cared little for others. But, although Edward would rather have a tooth pulled by a blacksmith than admit it, the gruff knight cared about the youth.

"Don't worry too much. We're still speaking to one another, unfortunately or not. I've known mules – and women – less stubborn. I suppose I even admire him, in a way. Although don't bloody tell him that. At least Thomas believes in something. I may end up sacrificing my life for this damned pilgrim, without believing in our so-called cause. Who's the more foolish then, between us?"

"Thomas is a strange bird, or fledgling," Emma said, fondly, platting part of her hair without even needing to look. Edward noted the dimples when she smiled fondly, and he thought how she appeared ten years younger. "I remember how Herleva once tried to catch his eye one evening. She was subtle at first, but bless him, Thomas was so innocent that he didn't realise the girl's intentions. He was uncommonly sweet and respectful, far more than she wanted him to be. But Herleva said that she liked him, which is more than she'll say about most men. And quite rightly too. Thomas told the sinner that he wanted to save her. But she replied that she just wanted to be paid for the services she offered – and with the money she could hopefully save herself. I fear that we all need saving now, from this Kerbogha and his army."

Despite the balmy air Emma shivered and the fond smile disappeared into the ether.

"Should Kerbogha attack, you must retreat immediately. You have your horse, although I am doing my best to get you a finer, faster mount. Ride in the opposite direction of the Turkish army. Don't look back. I will try to rendezvous with you, where we discussed. But if I'm not there you must forget about me and find a way home," Edward exclaimed. The gruff knight suddenly became affectionate, clasping the woman's hand – and gazing at her, drinking in her visage, as if it might be the last time he would see her.

"Escaping may be tantamount to a death sentence, or slavery. You will need every man – and woman – pulling together if there is a battle. I know how to handle a blade, better than most men. Certainly better than Thomas, it seems. I know where to hurt a man. Rumour has it that Bohemond has a plan to take the city, before we have to give battle. Instead of God, some people are praying to our prince to deliver us. Do you have a similar faith in Bohemond? Do you think we can lift the siege?" Emma asked, suspecting that Edward knew more about the plan than he was revealing.

"I'll believe it when I see it."

7.

The landscape was bone-dry, sucked clean of any beauty or nourishment. It was no longer the land of milk and honey, if indeed it ever had been. The silhouettes of the trees in the distance appeared like giant thorns. Thomas fancied that, should he reach out his hand, he would prick his fingers. If they were fruit trees, they would have lacked all fruit by now.

The sky was darkening, into a deep, glossy purple. The colour reminded Thomas of a set of robes which he had once seen Pope Urban wear. Yet somehow there was an absence of majesty and the divine, in both the firmament and the clergyman's garments.

The party of a dozen pilgrims closed in on the impoverished village. The wooden and stone structures seemed uncommonly brittle, as if a strong wind might blow them away. Erase the settlement from both the map and history.

Thomas wore his sword, to keep Edward happy. Whether out of guilt or not - or compelled by the fears the soldier had instilled in the non-combatant - Thomas spent part of the afternoon practising some of the sword strokes Edward and Owen had tried to teach him since the start of the siege. Thankfully the knight and scribe resumed their previous friendly relations, after their quarrel in the morning, when they met to disembark for their mission.

"I'd rather swallow bat's piss than swallow my pride and apologise, Thomas. I expect you feel the same. So, let's just agree to disagree. We've got enough enemies out there to deal with, without us fighting amongst ourselves," Edward remarked, taking the heat and awkwardness out of their encounter.

Thomas was all too willing to put their quarrel behind them too. Although the young Christian blanched at some of the knight's language and actions, he admired Edward. He was lowborn, but the soldier had made something of his life. He was also making surprisingly good progress learning his letters.

Edward and Hugh led the group, keeping a hawkish eye out for the enemy. There was every chance they could be mistaken for a foraging party and attacked. Advance scouts, from Kerbogha's army, could not be far away too. As well as keeping watch the two knights conferred with one another. Thomas occasionally caught snippets of their conversation. They joked about women and recalled drinking and roistering sessions.

"I could barely walk the next day. Constantinople – and the charms of the Byzantine courtesans – seemed like a dream even then. They're even more unreal now," Hugh remarked, as the knights reminisced. "Bohemond warned me that she was an agent of the scheming she-wolf, or she-cub, Anna Komnenos. He said that she would look to seduce and take advantage of me. But I like to think I took advantage of her, twice, that night."

"Beware of Greeks bearing gifts. But never look a gift horse in the mouth too," Edward replied. "Unfortunately, the courtesans in the Emperor's close circle didn't consider me important enough to bed and extract intelligence from. I had to head to the city's brothels and pay for it each evening. But we all end of paying for it, in some ways, in the end. More so if you end up spending your nights with a wife, as opposed to whore."

A small burst of laughter rang out in the desolate valley.

Thomas felt slightly jealous of the friendship between the two men. The young student had no one to share a joke with, not that he was in much of a mood to laugh. He enjoyed speaking with Bishop Adhemar, but their relationship was more akin to a teacher and student. Most of Bohemond's retinue considered him odd and gave him a wide berth. Non-combatants were almost regarded as non-people in the Norman army. Thomas permitted himself the briefest of wry smiles – blink and you would miss it – as he thought how Antioch was a home from home. Back in England the villagers had judged him to be "bookish" and "aloof". The scribe would translate that as being "strange".

The crossbow on Hugh's back caught Thomas' attention. He winced as he recalled the scene of a bolt slicing clean through a scrawny youth's stomach, during the Battle of Dorylaeum. The new form of weapon always caused him to shudder. Thomas imagined that, eventually, every soldier would carry a crossbow. Edward had argued that the weapons were too cumbersome and too slow to reload. "I've seen more than one man scythed down whilst attempting to fix a fresh quarrel onto the weapon and work its mechanism. There's the quick and the dead."

Thomas wasn't the only one who took in the crossbow. The three figures, waiting on their mounts, at the north entrance to the village, eyed the strange weapon too. Varhan stood in between two armed, pugnacious-looking attendants. His pitted skin was nut-brown. His off-white linen shirt and trousers could have once been considered fine - but were now frayed. Spindly fingers nervously played with an amulet around his neck. The merchant licked his dry lips and wiped his perspiring palms as he surveyed the party of westerners, visibly worried that they might cut him down at any moment. He tried to catch a glimpse of their teeth. Varhan had heard rumours that, due to starvation, some of the soldiers had become cannibals. They drank blood, having run out of wine, and ate the dead.

"Have you been sent by Bohemond?" Varhan said, gulping before speaking, addressing Hugh, who was dressed in the finest armour and riding the largest horse.

"Yes. Have you been sent by Firuz?" Thomas asked.

"Yes. I am Varhan. Please, follow me."

The Armenian wheeled his pony around and entered the village. He hadn't died yet or been threatened to be mutilated - or eaten. It was a good sign.

Thomas briefly found himself at the vanguard of his party. Edward soon put his horse into a trot and caught up with his countryman. The knight, whose first layer of armour was usually his indifference, was tense. He knew what was at stake. Failure did not bear thinking about. If they died on their mission, then so would the majority of the crusaders. Despite the waves of the desertions – and those who had perished through disease and starvation – the pilgrims still numbered in their thousands.

"If anything happens, stay close to me," Edward instructed Thomas. "Although what with all the bastards out there who want to kill me, remaining close to me may not prove the safest place. You could of course attempt to race away - but given that nag you're riding a cripple could well overtake you."

Thomas was barely listening to his friend, however. He was distracted by the reaction of the village to the soldiers. The settlers ushered themselves inside. Suspicion, fear and resentment reigned, as pervasive as a morning mist. Some of the villagers would look to hide what few valuables and provisions they owned. More than one mother shielded the sight of their daughters from the westerners. Thomas tried to offer up a concordant, reassuring smile to one mother but it was met by such a sour look that he fancied the expression could've curdled milk.

An emaciated dog padded past, followed by an elder crossing Thomas' path. For a moment or two their eyes interlocked. He could have been aged fifty or seventy, the Englishman considered. The old man was hunched over, as though half the world were pressing down upon him. He moved tentatively, as if each step caused him pain, using a walking stick which at any moment might snap. His joints creaked like the unoiled axles on an ancient cart. A forked, wispy beard hung down from a weak chin. The lines in his brow were cut deep, like scars. The stoical elder, who had survived both his wife and children, had seen the Franks take everything from the village in the past year. He had seen the Turks take everything from the village during previous years. The Turks would do so again, once the Franks had been defeated or when they moved on. Although Thomas was filled with compassion for the decrepit villager, it was the old man who possessed the more piteous expression for the pilgrim. The crusader was reminded of a piece of scripture. It was as though the elder was thinking, "Father, forgive them, for they know not what they are doing."

Thomas told himself that he would say a prayer for the infidel that night. Hugh didn't notice the scarecrow-like figure. Edward told himself to feel nothing for the villager, although he fleetingly fancied how the village could well be the eastern equivalent of his childhood home, back in England.

The sage, or demented old man, mouthed something to the young westerner. Thomas couldn't decide whether it was a blessing or a curse.

Varhan led the party to a crumbling stone cottage, with a thatched roof. The walls were strewn with vines, like varicose veins. Rags hung from a couple of over-burdened washing lines. A few weeds littered the space where there was once a vegetable patch and herb garden.

Varhan and Thomas exchanged a few words, which the latter translated for Hugh and Edward. The Armenian invited Thomas and the two knights inside the cottage. The remaining soldiers were asked to wait outside.

Their eyes were like two pairs of slits, set into a castle turret to shoot arrows out from. Henri and Girard peeked over the rocky ridge, which was set above the village. Their party, containing Girard's company of two dozen soldiers, set out earlier in the day to reconnoitre the area, in preparation for the arrival of Bohemond's men later in the day, in accordance with the intelligence Raymond received.

Girard's pulse had quickened when he spotted the English knight enter the village. His lips receded over his gums and his aspect was laced with malice.

He was tired of being tortured by images of Edward assaulting and defeating him. Humiliating him. Instead, he started to imagine slitting the Englishman's throat, as his men pinned his enemy down.

"We should attack immediately," Girard suggested, like a dog straining to be let off the leash. "We have the numbers. We have the element of surprise. Once we kill Bohemond's men we can capture Bohemond's contact. His plan can become our plan. Our gold will be as valuable as their gold."

Henri ground his teeth in reply. He had spent the day with the preening aristocrat – but it was enough for an entire lifetime. The knight bristled each time the nobleman opened his mouth. It was like having a fly buzzing next to his ear. His reedy, whining voice spewed out a litany of complaints throughout the afternoon. It was too hot. The wine was too diluted or not diluted enough. His armour had not been oiled and polished properly. Henri was also tired of the peacock's boasting about his horsemanship, his prowess as a lover and skills with a lance and sword. Girard's words ate away at the knight's patience, like rust eating away at a cheap blade.

The professional soldier ignored the man – whelp - next to him. He would order the attack when he was ready. The light may have been fading, but they needed to descend into the village under the cover of darkness. While there was some light, he would keep watch for any additional soldiers under Hugh's command. The ambushers should be wary of being ambushed themselves. Henri also needed to brief Girard's company. He hoped they were more accomplished soldiers than their leader. They needed to ensure they spared the Armenian and the young translator during the attack. Their strategy should also be to use the crossbowmen in their group to target Hugh and Kemp. They had the potential to turn the tide of a battle and rally their company. But they couldn't do so if dead.

Edward was pleased to take the weight off his feet. Such was his height, his head had been touching the low ceiling. His worry however was that the wooden chair that he was sitting on might collapse beneath him. The knight's nostrils tickled with a blend of smells. Cat's piss, mould and fresh bread.

The house belonged to Varhan's sister, Nazani. The lissom woman may well have been pretty in her prime, Edward estimated. But that prime was a long time ago. Time and life had worn her down, like the sea and wind eroding a cliff face. Her once glossy hair was now straw-like. Her once silky skin was now more akin to sackcloth. Nazani had not been the same since a Turkish raiding party, five years ago. When she was raped. One soldier had broken a finger on each of her hands and threatened to pour hot candle wax in her eye, so his victim didn't fight back. Nazani naturally felt apprehensive about inviting the western soldiers into her home. But her brother assured her all would be well. Firuz had promised his sister a significant bounty for helping to negotiate his deal with Bohemond – and Varhan had duly promised his sister a portion of his reward.

Varhan barked out some instructions for the woman to fetch some refreshments for their guests. His tone was more emollient when he addressed Thomas.

"You have something for me, yes?" the Armenian asked, following Firuz's suggestion to ask to see the gold first before commencing discussions.

"Yes," Thomas replied.

Hugh went outside and returned, carrying a small strongbox and heaving it on the table in front of Varhan. The gold coins shone as brightly as the surrounding flames on the candles in the room. And this was only part of the payment, he thought, resisting the urge to rub his hands together.

"And you have something for me?" Thomas asked. Bohemond had advised his translator to be polite, but direct.

"Yes, yes. This scroll contains a map and instructions for your commander to work with Firuz to take the city. I will also go through things now with you and answer any questions you have," the Armenian explained, before complaining to his sister that the flatbread she brought out wasn't warm enough.

Varhan worked his way through Firuz's plan, pausing every now and then to allow Thomas to translate things to the attentive soldiers. The two knights occasionally posed a question or offered a comment. They also nodded appreciatively at one another, approving of what they were hearing. The ruse had its merits and could work, which is not to say that it definitely would work. Few plans survive contact with the enemy. They would need a certain amount of good fortune for things to succeed, but God was on their side was He not? The knights were also aware that the plan involved placing a great deal of trust in their new confederate. There was ample scope for Firuz to betray his allies and ambush the crusaders. They would have to trust the traitor, because they had no choice. Edward realised that they needed to make a leap of faith. But the whole crusade was based on a gigantic leap of faith, he thought – either amused or in despair.

Hugh permitted himself a wry smile, after digesting the plan, along with his cold flatbread. Bohemond would approve of the clever ruse. The guileful and greedy Firuz may be a man after his own heart. After Thomas secured the scroll and started committing the details to memory Hugh stepped outside to check on his men. A few of his soldiers were sharing a wineskin or two. A couple carried oil lamps to illuminate the scene.

Varhan continued to engage with his guests as the Norman left the room.

"I want you to know that my friend is an honourable man. It is the despicable Yaghi Siyan who is a traitor to his people. He has stolen from them. He abuses them. Soldiers take wives and daughters from their homes and present them to the governor, like trophies, for his lascivious pleasure. Husbands and boys are forcibly recruited into the army. When you speak to your commander, the great and estimable Bohemond of Taranto, you must ask him to apportion some soldiers to protect my friend, Firuz."

"We will," Thomas dutifully replied.

"I must ask a favour of you too, on a personal matter. I have a niece, my late brother's daughter, still residing in Antioch. Yeva is a fine young woman. She has just suffered the misfortune, along with lots of young women, of marrying a bad man. He is a vile dog. A tyrant. He sleeps with whores and beats her. I must ask you to save my dear Yeva, when you enter the city. We both know what will happen if your soldiers find her. I have a map, marking where her house is in Antioch. I can pay you, once Firuz pays me. This is why I choose to help you, so Yeva would be safe. If you take care of Yeva for a few days, until it will be safe for me to enter the city again. You must say yes. Please," Varhan exclaimed, agitated, clasping Thomas' forearm in supplication, before impatiently barking out another order to his sister, to clear away the empty plates in the room.

"What's he saying now?" Edward asked, witnessing how animated the Armenian had become.

Thomas explained the situation. Edward rolled his eyes and then shook his head.

"No. We shouldn't get involved. Chivalry be damned. Tell him we cannot help," Edward asserted, keen to return to camp.

"If we can help, we should help. We both know what will happen if our soldiers sack the city. We already have enough blood on our hands. For once, we have a chance to deliver rather than damn someone. You are a knight, Edward. You have a sworn duty to defend the innocent."

"Don't talk so much bollocks. And don't tell me what my duties are as a knight. I can tell you that your duties as a translator don't involve making fanciful promises," the soldier replied.

Edward glanced at the Armenian. His bulbous eyes were unblinking. Pleading. Although Varhan was unable to understand what the Englishmen were saying he could tell they were disagreeing. He dropped to his knees in front of the knight and spoke in the westerner's native tongue.

"Please, help. Please, help."

Tears began to well in the Armenian's eyes as he gripped the knight's trousers. Edward pursed his lips and appeared awkward, embarrassed. He sighed, or harrumphed. He tried to appear sympathetic, whilst also flashing a look of scorn at Thomas for putting him in such a situation. The seasoned veteran would have rather been facing down an enraged Saracen than dealing with the sobbing foreigner, given a choice, Thomas suspected.

"God's blood. If you tell him that we will try to help his niece," Edward announced, but somewhat dismissively.

"Thank you, you are a good man, he says," Thomas conveyed, after exchanging a few words with the Armenian.

"Ha! He must have not diluted his wine. Next, he'll be saying that I have an honest face," Edward joked – but failed to smile.

Thomas said that they would endeavour to protect Yeva, although this did little to assuage Varhan's anxiety.

"Please, swear. Give me your word of honour. Both of you. Swear on your God. A knight's honour means something, no? You are a man of honour. You wear a cross. You are a man of God. Once you give your word, you must keep it. Honour is honour. Without honour, a man is nothing. He is a beast, dressed in finery," Varhan petitioned.

A pregnant pause hung in the air, like the insects buzzing around the light, as Thomas translated and waited for Edward to give his word of honour. But the words got stuck in his throat. He thought for one moment that they might choke him. The non-believer had never given his word of honour, with God as his witness, before. His oath shouldn't have meant anything to him. But somehow it did. He was conscious of the Armenian and Thomas gawping at him, in hope or expectation. Edward was reminded of a scene from his childhood. His mother's voice chimed in his ears.

"You should always keep a promise."

"Why?" Edward replied, curious.

"Because God is watching you."

Surely the Englishman could easily dismiss such an oath, as if he were just brushing away a cobweb in front of him. What did he owe to the Armenian? Or his niece, who he had never met? Who he would probably never meet. Even if this Yeva were as comely as Cleopatra he had Emma. He realised, perhaps at that very moment, that she was more than enough for him.

Edward finally, reluctantly, gave his word. He gasped for air afterwards, as if he were half-drowning. He felt like he had just made a pact with the devil. Or he had been marked with a branding iron. The knight was angry at Thomas, the Armenian and himself.

"Enough of this nonsense," Edward exclaimed, although Thomas diplomatically declined to translate this last sentiment. The knight did however thank Varhan for his service. He was tempted to say he would be rewarded in the next life for aiding the pilgrims, although Thomas suspected that the agent was more concerned with being rewarded in this one.

8.

Henri surveyed the scene, concealed behind a disused well. Girard was beside him. The nobleman swayed back and forth on the balls of his feet, as if he were standing on hot coals. Their men lay on the outskirts of the village, hidden in a trench, their faces daubed with dirt to further blend into the darkness. Some of them seemed understandably nervous, whilst others were champing at the bit. They wanted to get the fight over with and return to a campfire, wineskin and reward from Raymond of Toulouse.

Bohemond's soldiers were grouped outside a cottage, having recently been joined by Hugh of Cerisy. Edward Kemp, the translator and the contact they were meeting were inside. There were various angles of attack – but so too there were numerous escape routes for the enemy. Henri couldn't afford to allow anyone inside, or outside, the cottage to live. But he could afford to be patient.

Henri pictured the place where he intended to ambush Bohemond's men. It was a bottle neck. The rocky trail narrowed, running in between two shrub-filled slopes, where he could conceal his soldiers. He would first instruct his crossbowmen to target the Englishman and Hugh at the head of the party. They would then attack from the flanks and rear. The enemy would be clumped together, unable to fight back or escape. Horses would panic and throw their riders. They would be fish in a barrel. Henri would ensure that the translator lived. The ambush, as opposed to any attack in the village, would minimise losses to the company too.

The knight framed his thoughts. He would retreat up to the ridge, recover the horses and prepare his men for their surprise attack. The enemy would have no choice but to travel back through the pass. But at the same time that Henri settled on his plan Girard became increasingly unsettled. His blood boiled. The enemy were gathered together, ready to be slaughtered. Girard didn't know what the knight was waiting for. He drew his sword, as if to act as a prompt for Henri to give the order attack. But the soldier ignored the petulant nobleman. The whelp. Instead, the knight moved from his position to confer with a couple of men he had posted as sentries at the eastern mouth of the village. He ordered them to ready the horses.

"Are we not going to attack?"

"No, not now."

But Girard had other ideas, in the knight's absence. He briefed his company earlier that they should follow his orders, should there be a dispute between the two commanders. It was a sin against nature for the common soldier to try to supersede the nobleman's authority. Henri needed to learn his place in the order of things. Girard was born to lead. It was in his blood. He had been schooled in military strategy and tactics. He had read Caesar's *The Gallic Wars* and the first two chapters of *On Roman Military Matters*, by Vegetius. What had the illiterate Henri read? Girard mustered his men and ordered them out of the trench, guiding them through the village. The first wave of western soldiers forced the villagers inside. The second kept them inside.

The young aristocrat puffed out his chest and rested a hand on the pommel of his sword when issuing his orders, consciously imitating the stance his uncle often took when addressing his men. Girard decided to selflessly deny himself a portion of glory by declining to join the attack. He needed to keep his distance to orchestrate the offensive effectively, he argued. Thanks to Henri's caution, Girard would not be able to deploy any mounted troops – but the aristocrat believed that his contingent of crossbowmen would deliver victory. He positioned two sets of four crossbowmen either side of Bohemond's men. Another dozen or so members of his company were ready to advance from all sides, armed with swords and axes, within rushing distance of the enemy.

During the wait for his soldiers to move into position Girard pictured a wave of crossbow quarrels slamming into his foes. Felling them. He also imagined the words of praise and rewards his uncle would levy on him, when he proved successful in his mission. Such was his fervent belief in victory that Girard was blinded to the diffidence in the eyes of some of his soldiers, who were fearful of thrusting themselves into the heat of battle. Due to Girard's own reticence in testing himself against various enemies, many in his company were yet to be properly bloodied too.

The nobleman witnessed the Englishman exit the cottage, along with the translator and the contact they were meeting. It was a sign to commence his attack. God was on their side. Girard gave the order, by raising and then lowering his arm. A quartet of crossbowmen broke cover from behind an outbuilding, next to a ramshackle dwelling, Quarrels rested on their weapons, ready to be unleashed. On observing their counterparts in the distance, a second group of crossbowmen lined-up on the other side of Bohemond's men, appearing from out of nowhere like spirits from the underworld.

A series of shrill whooshing sounds laced the air, succeeded by horses whinnying. But the would-be deadly volley of missiles failed to kill anyone. Quarrels thudded into a couple of horses, but also struck the ground and whistled overhead. Confusion reigned in the treacly darkness. Bohemond's men were unsure who was attacking them, and how substantial a force it was. Could they be villagers? Turks? Shouts went up, but then dissipated like smoke. Raymond's men were unaware how unsuccessful their opening salvo had been. Girard's soldiers were now charging, on foot, a group of mounted troops.

Edward was one of the first to react decisively. He led Varhan and Thomas off around the side of the cottage, away from the crossfire, where he untethered his horse. The knight was met however by a couple of Girard's soldiers, barring his way like a couple of locked doors. The figure on his left grinned or grimaced, revealing a gap in his teeth which one could have slotted a prayer book through. The face next to him was buried in a bushy, greasy beard. One carried a short sword, the other a large mace. The Englishman duly noted how they were being attacked by Franks rather than Turks. Edward couldn't rely on Thomas or Varhan to enter the fray. But he wasn't without help. The knight drew his sword, before slapping the rump of his horse. The creature took a few quick steps forward and acted as a battering ram to break open the barrier in front of him. Before his enemies could re-orientate, Edward was on the front foot. The soldier, brandishing the short sword, drew his weapon back to slash at the Englishman, but Edward jabbed his own blade forward, skewering it into his gullet, emitting the word "Bastard!" as he did so. The point beats the edge. The Englishman pivoted in time to avoid the bloodstained mace's head staving in his skull. The weapon was powerful, but cumbersome. Before the bearded Frank could reset and swing the fearsome club again Edward swiped his broadsword upwards and sliced open his face, causing the gap between the soldier's teeth to further widen. A scream cut through the air like a winter chill, but the noise was drowned out by the roar and clang of battle. Edward, assisted by the Armenian's attendants, retrieved a number of horses – and he proceeded to lead Thomas and Varhan away from the skirmish. On more than one occasion the knight had to bellow instructions to the translator to spur him into action, from being frozen in fear. Edward didn't feel entirely comfortable abandoning his company and showing his back to the enemy – but it was of paramount importance that the plan, in some form, reached Bohemond. The entire campaign depended on it. After hearing the Armenian's strategy to capture the city, Thomas mentioned that their prayers could have been answered. Edward was more cautious, believing that there is many a slip between a cup and a lip.

Rather than concentrating on whether their missiles had hit the mark the crossbowmen focussed on reloading their weapons, straining to pull the drawstring back. As they did so however a slightly different kind of "whoosh" filled the air, succeeded by the noise of multiple thuds as Owen and his trio of archers entered the fight. Edward had ordered his friend to track their party from Antioch. Should they be attacked by bandits on the road to the village, then Owen and his men would ambush the ambushers. As soon as the English knight entered the cottage Owen had positioned himself on the roof of the empty stables, across from the dwelling. The Welshman permitted himself a grin, as he shot off his third arrow. The enemy had no idea where the murderous missiles were coming from. They were out in the open, exposed like a head on a block, waiting for an axe to fall upon them. Nock. Pull. Loose... Nock. Pull. Loose. He could hear his father's booming voice drill the three instructions into him. Owen had been a poacher since childhood. The prey had just changed. Killing was second nature. All manner of pandemonium was taking place around him but the archer methodically, murderously, went to work. The bowstring bit into his fingers, but not as stringently as the barbed arrowheads bit into flesh. Every one of his arrows hit its mark, even when the crossbowmen routed - and he aimed at moving targets.

Hugh steeled himself and the soldiers around him. He mounted his horse and squinted in the darkness, assessing the scene. Crossbow quarrels were lodged in the ground, rather than in his men. The sound of his archers unleashing their arrows was as welcome as a choir of angels. The spectres in the distance were falling to the ground, being sent back down to hell. Hugh couldn't entirely discern the strength of the enemy, but he judged that attack would be the best form of defence, as a wave of assailants closed in. He dug his heels into the flanks of his destrier and mowed down a brace of sword-wielding foes. Their ribs snapped and their heads split open like rotten fruit as they hit the ground. There were others who followed Hugh's lead and duly counter-attacked their opponents.

Henri heard the clash at arms at the heart of the village. Screams sliced through the stygian darkness. The knight let out more than one vociferous curse, suspecting that the whelp was at fault, as he rushed towards the fight. Perhaps he could help turn the tide of battle. But he soon dismissed such an idea. The battle was likely over, as Henri was confronted with a couple of familiar faces, retreating – being pursued by an enemy horseman. He cut Girard's men down, slashing his sword across their backs. Easy kills. Henri was determined not to lose his life as cheaply, as the enemy eyed his new target and spurred his mount on. Bohemond's man was surprised, but far from unhappy, that the foe was standing his ground. It would take less effort and energy to slaughter the brigand. The earth shook beneath him, as the horse closed in. Galloping. He noticed whirls of mist come out of its snorting nostrils, just before Henri feinted one way and dived the other. The horseman couldn't adjust his sword stroke in time. Before he had an opportunity to wheel his mount around for a second charge Henri rose to his feet, drew his dagger and launched it into his enemy. The blade easily pierced his leather jerkin. It may have even pierced a mail hauberk, should he be wearing one, such was the power of the throw. The rider fell from his horse like a sack of flour. Before he could pull the knife from his stomach Henri plunged his sword into his opponent's brain, through his eye socket.

The knight exhaled, emitting ten sighs in one, whilst quickly taking stock. Henri hadn't survived so many campaigns, without knowing when a battle was lost or won. He mounted the stray horse and rode for home. The soldier wanted to get back to camp. He looked forward to seeing his pet snakes again. He rightly trusted them over any man.

Girard didn't believe what he was seeing at first. Then he didn't want to believe it. He told himself he had surprise on his side - and he had the superior numbers - multiple times, like a refrain in a song. The scene was chaotic and confusing, cloaked in gloom. But, ultimately, he knew that the attack was failing. Or had failed. The lives of his men were being snuffed out, like a priest pinching and extinguishing candles at the end of mass. His breathing became irregular and his jaw increasingly dropped, like a man staring on, helpless, as he watched his home burning down in front of him. All the time, whilst gummed in a state of disbelief, Girard started to slowly walk backwards, fading into the darkness. Such was the frequency and ferocity of the arrows raining down on his men that he thought he was being attacked by forty, instead of just four, archers. As he began to breathlessly run through the village, away from the fight, the nobleman's next reaction to defeat was to curse the incompetence and cowardice of his men. They deserved to die, he concluded. Along with a trusted companion, Pierre, who he had whored and gambled with since his early adolescence, Girard put as much distance between the battle and himself as possible, disappearing into the wilderness. Eventually the bedraggled pair came across a farm, where they stole a couple of ponies. Thankfully Girard's confederate had studied a map of the region and was able to lead them back towards Antioch. Rather than dwell on any guilt - or mourn the loss of his men under his command - Girard focussed his mind on composing a narrative which would exonerate him in the eyes of his uncle. He thought that it would prove favourable if only he and Pierre returned from the mission. Indeed, he even offered up a prayer that God might help facilitate such a favourable outcome.

9.

Edward returned to Antioch in the dead of night. The embers of campfires were fizzling out. The last of any slurred drinking songs no longer carried through the air. Edward was soon followed by Hugh and the rest of their company. Bohemond was awake and greeted his soldiers. He was pleased that there had been no loss of life among his men. But he was far more concerned – and happier – about the news that the meeting with the Armenian went well. Bohemond devoured the contents of the scroll, as if it were a letter from his wife – or mistress. He nodded, grunted and finally grinned in response to its contents. He occasionally asked a pointed question, but Bohemond was satisfied. Or as satisfied as Bohemond could be. The plan was secured, and workable. Their mission had been a success – and success should be rewarded, he believed. The prince arranged wine and roasted meats for his men and invited Edward, Hugh and Thomas into his tent.

Bohemond heaped praise on his translator for his work. When he clapped Thomas on the shoulder the youth's legs nearly gave way. Without the scribe, he would not now be in the position to take the city. He acceded to Thomas' request to give him a large portion of the money he was safekeeping for him – in order to pass on the coin to Adhemar to distribute food to the neediest pilgrims.

"You have more steel in you than you might realise lad. You must have acquitted yourself well," Bohemond stated, in a more convivial tone than usual. "You now have a taste for battle, eh?"

Thomas was too tired or frightened to contradict the figure who towered over him.

"God will reward your service in the next life, but I shall try to reward you in this one. You have earned the honour of being part of the force who will storm the city. I may have need of your talents as a translator during and after the attack."

Thomas didn't feel particularly honoured and was unable to thank his prince. As much as his heart was flooded with fear by the prospect of storming the city, he realised that he needed to do so if he was to keep his promise and save Yeva. Thomas had given his oath, like a knight-errant. To break his word would be a grave sin. He shuddered at the thought. He also shuddered at the thought of joining a forlorn hope.

Bohemond turned his attention next to Edward and Hugh, who proffered a more detailed account of the engagement.

"They were Franks, as opposed to Turks. I didn't recognise anyone, but I'd be willing to wager that they were Raymond's men," Hugh argued. "Unfortunately, it's difficult to interrogate the dead."

"If the bastards were able to shoot a crossbow properly then you'd be giving out funeral orations rather than jugs of wine," Edward added.

Bohemond scratched his beard and his eyes narrowed. He used his thumb to turn a ring on his finger, given to him by his father, as if he were turning cogs in his mind. Wheels within wheels. Although it was often difficult to divine what the Norman was thinking, it was clear that he was thinking – which one couldn't necessarily make the claim for in relation to other noblemen. Others might have asserted that Bohemond was always scheming, instead of thinking, if they were being uncharitable.

"It doesn't surprise me, that Raymond would act in such a dishonourable manner. It's further evidence that he cares more for his own interest than he does for the campaign," Bohemond pontificated, without a flicker of irony. "The man is not fit to lead a pack of brigands, let alone knights. I need to be disappointed, as opposed to vengeful, however. Even if I could provide cast iron proof of his involvement and guilt, I would have to tread carefully. Or step back from accusing him. I may not need Raymond, but I do need his army still to secure the city. It's now the case though where I trust the Muslim convert traitor, Firuz, over my supposed Christian brother. You should always think the worse of people – and then you will never be betrayed by them. The world may not be an inherently wicked place – although nature is prone to savagery and selfishness – but it is populated with wicked people. But not everyone is wicked. You trusted this Varhan, did you not?" Bohemond asked Edward.

"I'm not sure if I wholly trust anyone. In my experience horses and dogs can be trusted, but not men. The Armenian seemed sincere though, or he is an even more accomplished actor than I am a seasoned drinker. He even petitioned us to save his niece, once we're inside the city."

"If Varhan can be trusted, then I'm further assured that we can trust his confederate inside the city. Firuz's plan is audacious, but not without merit. We must submit to it. We do not have time to organise an alternative strategy, before Kerbogha graces us with his presence. We must do or die," Bohemond determined, his taut features hardening even more. He appreciated however how fatigued his men must be. Edward appeared so haggard that he feared the knight's skin might fall from his face like melting wax. The prince proceeded to dismiss his soldiers.

Whilst Edward and Thomas plunged themselves into sleep, their bodies feeling like one large bruise, Bohemond remained awake. He prowled around his chamber, like a tiger in a cage, his head bowed, as if in prayer. He was so close to realising his ambition – solidifying a dream. The prince recalled his visit to the Church of Santa Sophia in Constantinople. He was nearly blinded by the polished marble floors and vaunting columns, leading up to a spacious and majestic domed ceiling. One felt like one's voice could reach up to heaven. Shafts of pristine, amber light poked through the windows – like the fingers of God. The building was awe-inspiring, a monument to God, engineering and art. Breath-taking. Faith giving. The church was the jewel in the crown of Constantinople. A sense of humility and grace came over Bohemond, as much as Bohemond could ever feel grace and humility. The pungent aroma of incense stirred his noble nostrils and soul. If ever God was going to listen to the Norman, he believed it would be here. The hulking soldier removed his sword and fell to his knees. But not to pray. He did not ask God to help him in his desire to become king of Antioch or Jerusalem. Rather, he told the Almighty what his intentions were – and that even if God disapproved of his actions, Bohemond would defy Him and still fulfil his destiny. He would cut down every last man between Constantinople and Antioch, like a forester hacking through a dense wood, if he had to. The Christian prince also resolved that Constantinople should be his ultimate goal. But one step at a time. He was only a mere mortal, rather than deity, unfortunately. Alexios, as opposed to Kerbogha, was his ultimate enemy. Bohemond knew that the Emperor didn't trust him. He knew that he detested him. But the Norman would one day wipe the superior smile off the Byzantine's perfumed face.

Bohemond had spent the rest of that day travelling around the wondrous, prosperous city in a state of ambition and admiration. Constantinople was home to the largest hippodrome he had ever seen, an array of churches, bathhouses, markets and a zoo. The Emperor's spies followed him. Bohemond knew he was being followed. Partly the commander was mapping the city and noting its strategic strengths and weaknesses. He cast his eye over the Blachernae Gate, fastened with iron bolts and guarded with two flanking crenelated towers, manned with archers. Not even Joshua could bring down such walls, his nephew, Tancred, had commented. But one day Bohemond would return, with a more powerful army. As Robert Guiscard had once disclosed to his young son, "No one will ever give you anything for free in this world. You have to take things, by might or guile." The famed city was almost impregnable. *Almost.*

Morning.

The dawn glowed, as much as the Count of Toulouse's bloodshot - from rage and wine - eyes. The mission had been an abject failure. Raymond was still no wiser as to the details of Bohemond's strategy to procure the city - and still no closer to taking it from him. The skirmish had been a waste of good men, men that he could ill afford to lose. He cursed his nephew. This campaign was supposed to make a man of him. But the prince was not an alchemist. He couldn't turn lead - or shit - into gold. Only his affection for the boy's mother prevented Raymond from ordering his hunting hounds to tear him limb from limb - or running his sword through the youth. Or he could have easily ordered Henri to remove his nephew from the world. The knight would have done so with pleasure. Not even a hammer and chisel could alter the scowl on the furious soldier's face. Henri may have also relished the prospect of digging the grave or tossing the corpse on a burning pit himself.

Girard stood before his uncle once more. In disgrace. A failure. Awaiting punishment. A couple of men from his company had returned from their mission - and had shown as much loyalty to Girard as he had shown to them. Raymond had asked them to report on the disastrous events which occurred in the night:

"Tell the truth. If I suspect that you are lying to me, it'll be the last words you utter."

The fatigued, injured soldiers provided an alternative version of how the mission imploded, which contradicted Girard's version. The nobleman was responsible for the attack. The nobleman was responsible for the defeat. When confronted with the truth, in the presence of both Raymond and Henri, Girard broke down and pleaded for forgiveness. His crime was wanting to succeed. To serve. If only his crossbowmen would have hit their targets, they would be celebrating rather than censuring him right now, Girard argued. His men had let him down. Words and excuses poured out of him, like diarrhoea, Henri judged.

"A bad workman blames his tools. Your men behaved with ten times more honour than you displayed. If only one of the stray quarrels would have went so awry, as to cut you down, as you remained outside the fight. But there doesn't seem to be that much justice in the world, divine or otherwise," Raymond flatly remarked, unstinting in his condemnation. "Your company is forfeit. Your wealth is forfeit. Your brother was right to disinherit you. There are cowards and thieves belonging to Peter the Hermit's rabble who possess more honour than you."

Raymond became sick to his stomach of looking upon his wretched nephew - and dismissed him from his sight. As Girard made his way out of the chamber, what little composure Raymond maintained was abandoned - and the prince comically spouted a litany of curses at the nobleman whilst launching various pieces of food and cutlery at his back.

"Family! You can't live with them - and one can't always execute them," the prince stated, humourlessly. "Girard is the least of my concerns, however. It is likely that Bohemond knows that we were behind the attack on his men. He may be out for blood - or may look to publicly condemn me. If required,

I will claim that Girard's company, tired of his degenerate habits and poor leadership, deserted. I can argue that they attacked Bohemond's men independently. It is not uncommon for pilgrims to behave like brigands and steal from their own. I suspect that Bohemond will keep the events of last night quiet. He will want to plough ahead with his plan - and he will not be able to do so if he causes ruptures within the Council of Princes. But let us address such issues, if or when they arrive. You must be tired, my friend. I am grateful for your service, as usual. Get some rest and we shall speak later."

Henri was tempted to offer his prince some words of support or consolation, but he was too weary or indignant. The knight felt that the prince should have punished his nephew more severely. If it was up to him, the mercenary would have slit the youth's throat and let him bleed out, so the last thing he heard was his own death rattle. Henri merely pursed his lips, perhaps biting his tongue as he did so, and took his leave.

Raymond dismissed a couple of obsequious attendants who entered, requiring instructions on an array of subjects, and slumped upon his iron chair. He offered up a few curses, directed towards his nephew, Bohemond and the world in general, before puffing air out of his cheeks in exasperation. And then he growled. As did his stomach. The joints in his knees cracked. Time was catching up with the powerful magnate. There were occasions, before the infernal campaign, when the count boasted that he felt half the age he was. Now he sometimes felt that he was twice the age he was. Raymond mused how he could often split logs with his axe with just a couple of strokes. Now it took three or four blows. As a younger man he could, like a young Caesar, run and leap onto the back of his horse. It had been decades since he had attempted such a trick, for fear of making a fool of himself in front of his men. It was not just important that he gain the respect of the world in this life. The warrior and nobleman wanted his fame to outlive him, after his cold body had been buried in the ground. Raymond wanted his name to endure for as long as the marble statue of himself, brandishing his sword and shield, with his crest emblazoned on the front, at his castle in Toulouse. His achievements should live on - and not just through the chronicles and poems he had commissioned writers to produce.

His victories had been numerous, from his home in Provencal to the Levant. The count was feared and respected in equal measure. The peasantry of Toulouse revered him - prayed for him. Raymond had garnered a list of titles throughout his life, but the prince still wasn't a king. Even Baldwin called himself king now. Bohemond was aiming to do the same. Raymond bristled at the prospect and balled his hand into a fist, whilst grinding his teeth. He had joined the crusade with the intention of becoming king of Antioch or Jerusalem. Or both. Regret pinched him again. Before committing to the cause, he should have demanded being given overall command of the armies of God. He possessed leverage, back then. Urban and Adhemar had exploited him - when, usually, the Count of Toulouse was accustomed to exploiting others.

God had blessed and protected him all his life. But had his sins, like time, finally caught up with him? God had abandoned, disinherited, the prince. Raymond's young son had died during the campaign and he had lost the devotion of his wife, Elvira. She didn't say anything to openly defy or undermine him. But she didn't need to.

The powerful Frank had sacrificed everything for the cause. But all was not lost. Raymond thought about an aged boxer, he had once seen, floor a young challenger. The iron-haired warrior still had some fight left in him. If he couldn't procure the city, he still might be able to capture and claim the citadel, which looked out over Antioch like an eagle surveying its territory. Bohemond would be all too aware of the eyrie's strategic importance. He would devote a certain portion of his forces to secure the fortress. Raymond would do the same. It would be a race. A bloody one.

More than Kerbogha, Raymond considered Bohemond to be his chief enemy. He wasn't alone in such a judgement. Recognising that they shared a mutual enemy, Raymond and Alexios allied themselves with one another. Bohemond had declared war on his own brother in the past. There was reason to believe he would eventually betray the Byzantines and pilgrims. Raymond recalled his meeting with the Emperor, during his first night at the Blachernae Palace. Alexios had invited the Frank, wearing both a sword and surplice, into a chamber filled with tribute for the prince. Raymond squinted at the sight of ornate, bejewelled weapons, finely crafted diadems, a glittering array of coins and sparkling baubles, which appeared like ripened fruit, waiting to be plucked.

"For the greatest of western princes, we must grant the greatest treasure," Alexios smoothly remarked, smiling. "'Tis a gift, rather than a bribe, of course. Unlike your fellow noblemen, I will not compel you to swear an oath of fealty. I trust you. You have proved yourself to be a man of honour and a man of God."

Raymond nodded in reply. He knew that the politic leader was flattering him - but he indulged his generous host.

"As you know, rulers must serve too. I heard a calling - and took the cross."

"If only I could believe that all in your party were as honourable as yourself. You share my concerns, I believe," Alexios exclaimed, knowing that the westerner did, as his spies had intercepted his guest's correspondence. "We have a mutual goal, of liberating Jerusalem and expelling the Turks from our territories. But we also possess a mutual enemy, in Bohemond.

He is his father's son, a serpent of the devil's brood. I have no doubt that the faithless Norman will break his oath, as surely as the scorpion stung the frog in Aesop's fable. Yet Bohemond will wait till he crosses the river, before striking. You are the only man in a position to challenge and rein in the warmonger. Robert of Normandy is honourable and pious but lacks military prowess. Godfrey lacks your authority and leadership skills. Adhemar possesses the power to charm instead of command. The former is a laudable trait for a diplomat, but to be a soldier one must exhibit the latter. The bishop is a fine preacher and philosopher - I have much enjoyed his urbane company - but he is no military leader. I have the utmost respect for your pontiff, but Urban made a grave mistake by not investing you with overall command of the campaign. The armed pilgrimage should not suffer - or perish - for the error. We both know that popes can be fallible, as all men are fallible," Alexios argued, although he failed to mention whether emperors were fallible too.

"What's past is past. We must look to the future now."

That evening, Raymond and Alexios formed a delicate alliance. The Byzantine emperor promised the Frankish nobleman untold riches should he help him secure Antioch and Jerusalem for the glory of God and the empire. Raymond presented his host with a ceremonial sword, which he claimed belonged to Charlemagne. Alexios offered his guest the use of his chief mistress – and a Bible rumoured to have once been the property of Louis the Pious. The two powerful men told themselves that they were bringing together the best of the East and West. The armed pilgrimage could just be the start of a new era of cooperation. The days of Turkish expansion were numbered. There would no longer be a great schism between the two Christian realms. Anything was possible. The future seemed bright, for one brief moment.

That balmy evening was a lifetime ago, however, Raymond despondently thought, as he tried to prop himself up on his chair. Before the siege of Nicaea and battle at Dorylaeum. Before Baldwin's self-serving campaign. Before the weeping sore of Antioch. Before the death of his son. Sometimes Raymond would stare in private, in a maudlin fashion, at a portrait he had commissioned of his son. His innocent son. The artist had captured his impish expression and wide, bright aspect - full of curiosity and wonder. But at other instances the boy's father could not even bring himself to be in the same room as the painting. The image or memories made his eyes, or soul, burn.

What had his ally sacrificed? What had Alexios lost? Even when establishing a spirit of cooperation Raymond had little intention of delivering up the prizes of both Antioch and Jerusalem to the decadent Emperor. Raymond often pictured Alexios, wearing make-up, ogling his courtiers or ruminating on how he could exploit friends and enemies alike. Everyone else in the world was born to serve the semi-divine Emperor. To amuse him. To praise him. To toil for him. To fight for him. But the Frank, once he was in possession of Antioch, would not then surrender it to the self-serving Byzantines - especially as it was now likely that the armies of God wouldn't reach Jerusalem. The Holy City seemed even further away now than when the count sat by his hearth back in Provencal and first corresponded with Urban about the campaign. The crusade. The doomed crusade.

10.

Raymond of Toulouse insisted that the meeting of the Council of the Princes take place at a venue of his choosing. If the other princes could not assent to his request, then he would not attend.

"As he knows that he will never be King of Antioch, Raymond is pitching for the slightly less prestigious role of Lord of Pettiness," Bohemond remarked to Adhemar, after hearing the news. His first instinct was to defy and frustrate his fellow noblemen. But the meeting had to happen as soon as possible. They needed to attack the city now, or never. Adhemar only told Bohemond what he already knew, when he argued to permit that Raymond have his way.

"I am not yet fully apprised of your plan, but I suspect that you will still need his army to capture the city. I would recommend that you allow Raymond this small victory, in the pursuit of fulfilling your larger triumph."

Bohemond pretended to be torn in his decision, to stress his sense of compromise and sacrifice, but he finally gave his assent. He also duly flattered Adhemar, on his powers of diplomacy: "And I thought God moved in mysterious ways."

The Council of Princes had gathered regularly, since leaving Constantinople. The noblemen would come together to resolve military issues, the perennial topic of feeding their armies and other logistical conundrums. There were always plenty of problems – and far fewer solutions – to address between the armies of God. Thankfully Adhemar, who led the Council, was a voice of calm and conciliation, in the face of the often fractious and vain-glorious noblemen, who could squabble like children and take offence quicker than a whore could drop her dress. The bishop had lost count of the amount of times he had healed rifts and soothed someone's wounded pride. His tactic was to speak to each prince with a grievance individually – and try to engineer a compromise whereby both parties believed they had won the dispute, or at the very least had not lost it. Adhemar was also conscious of representing and championing the pilgrims on their campaign who were non-combatants. Bohemond would often call them "parasites" or "holy fools" but the bishop referred to them as "souls."

Next to Adhemar, Raymond had often steered and dominated the Council of Princes during the first half of their campaign. He was fond of reminding the other princes, subtly or otherwise, that he possessed the largest army and treasury out of the group. But the Count of Toulouse no longer commanded the respect of the group as he had once done. The princes increasingly looked to Bohemond for leadership. He had proved himself in battle – and now he was the only one proposing a plan to take the city they had been besieging, bootlessly, for over six months. It hadn't happened overnight, that Bohemond had usurped Raymond's authority – but it had happened.

"A small victory is still a victory," Raymond remarked to Adhemar, after the bishop had given him the news that Bohemond and others would defer to his decision to host the meeting in the main chamber of his billet. He was less pleased however with the Norman keeping him waiting, when the rest of the participants had assembled.

Adhemar, Robert of Flanders, Godfrey of Bouillon, Tancred de Hauteville and Robert of Normandy were already present, waiting with a mixture of anticipation and impatience for Bohemond to arrive. Incense infused the room. Stubs of candles flickered on the walls.

Bohemond sent Hugh, Edward and Thomas ahead. He instructed his knights to assess the mood of the chamber and, once the meeting commenced, to note the reactions and interactions between the attendees.

"Keep an eye on Raymond and my nephew. The two have been courting one another - or may have even consummated their alliance. We de Hauteville's are not to be trusted. Raymond may purchase his loyalty, if he hasn't already done so. Tancred is keen to make a name for himself and fulfil his ambitions, even if he has to ruin mine to do so… But I also want you to note Godfrey. I warrant that I can sway Robert of Normandy – and Robert of Flanders will be up for the battle ahead. I still do not know if Godfrey will support my proposal, however. Is he deeply devout, or does he just want to appear so? Antioch is of secondary importance to him. He is keen to march on to Jerusalem, like a fly attracted to shit. I worry that he may be a man of his word and desire to deliver up the city to our munificent emperor… I need to know who's for me or against me."

Edward was only too glad to oblige his prince when he saw the food, wine and ales their host laid out on a banquet table. His assignment was a damn sight less arduous – and perilous – than his previous mission, he reasoned. Edward was keen to attend the gathering as he rightly judged that Henri of Bayeux would be present. The Englishman wanted to confidently look the Norman in the eye. Challenge him. Whether Henri appeared innocent or guilty Edward would consider him guilty, in relation to being behind the attack yester night. Earlier in the afternoon Edward had tracked down one of the men posted on the camp's cordon – and he reported how Henri had left the camp the night before with Girard of Mortain and a force of twenty or so soldiers.

In contrast to his countryman, Thomas appeared ill at ease as he stood in the corner and watched as the room began to fill up with princes, each accompanied by a few senior knights.

Intimidating and imposing. The tension in the room would have been palpable to a blind man. It was as if they were all standing in a pool of naphtha, each of them holding a taper that might drop at any moment. Thomas bit his nails and chewed the skin on the inside of his mouth, worried that Bohemond might call upon him to address the whole council. He gulped, imagining the likes of Raymond barking orders at him, to clarify a point or speak up.

"Do you know why Bohemond has bid us to attend?" Thomas asked Edward, as they walked towards Raymond's camp.

"I find it best not to ask too many questions, lad, as I often don't like the answers."

Thomas was temporarily distracted from his anxious thoughts however, as he overheard part of a conversation between Tancred de Hauteville and Robert of Flanders, who were standing close by. Thomas didn't need to consult the Delphic Oracle to know that the two princes were discussing Stephen of Blois.

"It was his wife who ordered him off to go on campaign – and his wife who ordered him back. His is more wife-fearing than God-fearing," Tancred asserted, as if he were sucking on a lemon. The two princes were among the youngest taking part of the crusade, yet the campaign had aged them and hardened their hearts, like a date drying out in the sun. "If the shrew asked him to thrust his sword up his arse, he would reply "How far?" We are no worse off without the caitiff – the sheep in wolf's clothing - but we would be better placed if he hadn't taken others in his army with him. There will be a special alcove in hell for him when he dies – and hopefully he'll only have his wife for company during eternity."

Robert of Flanders motioned to reply, no doubt wishing to heap further opprobrium on the dishonourable nobleman, but out of the corner of his eye he spotted Bohemond enter the chamber.

Questions would now be answered.

Herleva pursed her lips and let out a sigh, or un-lady-like snort, of frustration. The young whore had all but run out of the kohl she used to line her almond eyes. The lack of make-up was a further sign that they should return home.

Emma sat in the tent with her most profitable girl. Even without make-up Herleva would have been considered twice as desirable as the other girls in her stable, the madam fancied. She could wear a miller's sack for a dress, but punters would still discern the quality of her figure and assets. Even if her regulars discovered that she might have the pox, they would still want to be with her. Herleva had left home and her drunken, abusive father after her mother died, when she was fifteen. She took to the trade like a duck to water, knowing when to dominate or subjugate herself, depending on the demands of different clients. She rightly derived more pleasure from making money than having sex. No matter how much Emma kept putting up her prices, her regulars – knights, noblemen and priests - remained loyal, enamoured.

The madam continued to go through the list of clients who owed her money, for services rendered by her girls. Edward had recently helped her collect her debts, as the no-nonsense Englishman threatened to cut off fingers, or other parts of their anatomy, if they refused to pay their dues.

"It must be time to leave this godforsaken place," Herleva suggested to her friend, not for the first time in the past fortnight or so. The enemy were coming. She had heard rumours of how the Turks mistreated women. She could be raped or sold into slavery. Or both. "Bohemond has bigger things to worry about. He hopefully won't notice or care we've left. We could go back to Constantinople on our way home. We could spend the day shopping and nights working. What's keeping you here?"

Emma was going to answer "Edward," but she didn't want to admit to her friend how much the Englishman meant to her – or admit to herself how much she liked the knight. The madam had always cautioned her girls against falling for any of their clients. She felt a slight professional embarrassment at failing to follow her own advice.

"We will leave soon. We will not stay too long," Emma stated, vaguely.

"We may already have stayed too long. We've squeezed what we can out of the commoners and nobles. There's no money or food left. The well has run dry. I must have slept with everyone in the camp," Herleva argued.

"Not everyone, of course," the madam replied, playfully, arching an eyebrow. "Young Thomas still seems immune to your charms. He may as well be a eunuch. I have seen you talking to him on more than one occasion. He still hasn't put his hand in his pocket for you though, so to speak. There must be something wrong with him," the madam said, amused by the situation.

"He's different to others here, which means there may be something right about him. Don't laugh, but I like him. He's decent. He looks me in the eye, instead of looking at just my tits, when he talks to me. But I am not going to let you change the subject that easily. We need to discuss when we are going to leave," Herleva insisted, hoping that if they did so they would be accompanied by Edward – and Thomas.

"It's not safe to leave right now."

"But it must be even less safe to stay."

Raymond had modified the chamber, in light of the important gathering. Banners were hung from walls, along with portraits of the host. A Bible lay open on a lectern, close to the count's great, iron chair. A tapestry, charting the history of his family – and his own triumphs – was mounted behind the mock throne. Various knights and attendants stood against the walls, their backs arrow straight. The prince aimed to project a sense of power, wealth and religious observance.

Adhemar and Raymond sat at either end, joint heads of the table. The other princes sat on long benches, facing one another, winecups in front of them. Adhemar had taken the serving staff aside beforehand and instructed them to dilute the measures. The bishop didn't want the wine to pour oil onto the fire of any heated discussions.

Bohemond had confidently and cordially greeted his fellow princes when entering. He had prepared a few opening lines and uncontentious topics of conversation for each nobleman, aside from Raymond. The two men frequently glanced at one another, yet also acted as if they didn't exist.

As per his routine, before giving a sermon, Adhemar took a sip of wine to wet his lips – and then took a breath whilst briefly closing his eyes to centre himself. Bohemond was impressed by the way that the bishop always came off as seeming serene rather than sanctimonious. The clergyman thanked the table for attending the meeting at such short notice. He proceeded to update the princes on recent intelligence reports and information about supplies of provisions, as dire as the news was.

"You may have sent out your own scouts, but my agents have advised me that the enemy will be upon us in three days. And that Kerbogha's army is three times the size of ours. We should not underestimate the quality and quantity of the enemy forces. Although Baldwin was successful in resisting Kerbogha, he was able to do so behind formidable city walls. We are on the wrong side of Antioch's defences at the moment, but we could be on the right side of them by the time our foes arrive. As you may already know, Bohemond has liaised with an ally in the city. I will allow him to explain."

Adhemar nodded towards the imperious prince and sat down. Bohemond stood up, towering above everyone, brushing some non-existent crumbs from his purple surcoat. He was accustomed to giving speeches and being the centre of attention. Rather than address his audience at the table he walked a few paces and stood at an invisible pulpit. He consciously positioned himself behind his host. At first Raymond craned his neck - but he then submitted to turning his chair and facing his rival, grunting as he did so.

Bohemond explained how he intended to lead a sizeable detachment of knights and infantryman away from the city, in sight of the enemy, tomorrow afternoon. The garrison would hopefully be fooled into believing that the crusaders were finally retreating, in response to the threat of Kerbogha's arrival. The force however would double-back under the cover of darkness. A vanguard of knights would rendezvous at the part of the wall entrusted to their Armenian contact. A rope would be lowered and attached to a ladder, for the knights to scale and enter the city. The soldiers would secure a couple of watchtowers and then open the Gate of St George, for reinforcements to enter the city.

"It is the best plan we have, because it is the only plan we have," Bohemond concluded.

"How do we know that we will not be led into a trap? How can we trust this Firuz?" Robert of Flanders asked.

"You will have to trust me," Bohemond said, assuredly.

A few of the princes and knights in the room shared a look, as if they were waiting for one another to offer up a satirical or cynical comment. But it didn't come.

"I am going to put my faith in Firuz, so you will not have to," Bohemond added. "I will personally volunteer myself and my men to scale the ladder and enter the city. If God favours us, Antioch will be given into our hands."

"Our hands?" Raymond exclaimed, scoffing. "You say that Antioch will be ours, but what you really mean is that Antioch would be yours, according to the terms of the agreement you proposed during our last council. I must protest again and remind everyone of the oaths they gave to the Emperor. I believe you to be honest men – and that you do not wish to throwaway your honour, like a drab throwing away her virtue. God will not favour us if we act as faithless as heathens and we break our contract with our ally."

"Our ally broke his contract with us. It has already been annulled. Alexios promised he would resupply and reinforce us. But where is he? He is probably still back in Constantinople, sodomising some eunuch with the traitor Tatikios looking on. And have you forgotten Nicaea? We spilled our blood and guts during the siege, only for him to sweep in at the end like a harpy, negotiate the surrender and steal our prize. We are not the ones who lack a sense of honour or courage. We all realise how we have been fooled and exploited by the Byzantines. We fight for them rather than with them. Instead of princes, Alexios regards us as mere sell-swords. We have more than earned any baubles he gifted us in Constantinople. We owe him nothing now. Alexios has abandoned us. We should duly abandon him," Bohemond contested, as though the argument had already been won. He was also keen to sow seeds of division against the Emperor, which would hopefully bear fruit at a later date – in the form of a crusade to capture the Byzantine capital. Bohemond had already whispered into the ears of some of his fellow princes that Alexios' ultimate aim might be to travel west instead of east, whilst their lands remained undefended.

Edward noted that there was more nodding than shaking of heads among the other princes – although the Englishman sensed that their minds had been made-up even before Bohemond had opened his mouth.

"Are you so sure that Alexios has forsaken us?" Raymond asked, pouncing. The count saw a chink in his rival's armour, a trap he could fall into. One of Raymond's agents had assured him that morning that Alexios was leading a relief army. Although the agent would not commit to saying that the Byzantines would arrive before Kerbogha's forces, they were on their way. Alexios hadn't abandoned them.

"I am sure," the stolidly built Norman replied. Resolute. "You have more chance of seeing Alexios turn up on a unicorn, with the Golden Fleece draped over his shoulders, clasping the Shield of Achilles, than you have of seeing him turn up on time."

"Then you will not be averse to agreeing to taking stewardship, rather than ownership, of Antioch should Alexios keep his word? As we must not then break our oaths with him. We swore our fealty before God," Raymond remarked, citing an authority that even Bohemond would not dare to openly defy. "Should you be so sure of our ally betraying us then you will have no qualms about submitting to such an arrangement."

"I agree," Robert of Normandy asserted, his voice as clear as his position.

"I agree too," Godfrey echoed, although there was a catch in his throat as he spoke. The Christian felt ill at ease, thinking that he might somehow break a sacred oath. God would punish him, in this world or the next.

Bohemond forced a smile and paused. He narrowed his eyes, calculating the odds. For once, did Raymond know something he didn't? He could not now waver or delay. The plan was set for tomorrow evening. It was do or die. If Raymond withdrew his support, then others might follow. He did not have the numbers to capture the entire city. Even Tancred might side with his rival – but at least that might reveal where his nephew's loyalties resided. Curse them all he thought to himself, whilst craving their blessing.

"Adhemar, you are in constant correspondence with the Byzantines," Robert of Normandy remarked, filling the stale silence. "Can we trust our allies? Will the Emperor come to our aid?"

The bishop furrowed his brow and appeared even more philosophical than usual. His stroked his chin and replied:

"I believe that Alexios intends to honour his word. We should pray for his appearance – and our deliverance – but for pragmatic reasons we should plan as if the Byzantines will not arrive in time. Therefore, I endorse Bohemond's proposition. We must attack the city tomorrow night. However, Raymond is also right. We should agree to grant stewardship, as opposed to ownership, of the city to Bohemond, should our allies prove true to their word," Adhemar suggested, hoping that he had satisfied - or had at least half-satisfied - both rival princes. Euclid might disagree, the studious bishop wryly thought to himself, but occasionally in politics it was possible to square a circle.

There was consensus in the council to concur with Adhemar. Bohemond nodded in assent - and donned an air of nobility and magnanimity, like he was laying a crown upon his head, in response to the bishop's proposal.

"I must insist that we continue with my contingency planning. Kerbogha will be with us in three days. I predict that he will mount his attack from the Iron Bridge. We should fortify the structures there. We will be able to bottleneck their forces and slow their momentum. You will forgive me, Bohemond, if I do not attach the same value to your plan and Armenian that you do," Raymond stated, forcing a polite or politic smile, behind the gaol of his gritted teeth.

"Someone values my plan it seems though, I warrant, as my men were attacked when they met with the Armenian's agent yesternight. The brigands could well have encountered my soldiers by accident, but I suspect that they were there to intercept the intelligence. But there isn't any reason why you should know anything about that, is there?" Bohemond posed, with a telling look and inflexion in his voice.

11.

With every breath, or blink of an eye, Adhemar seemed to fluctuate between hope and despair as he collected his thoughts, after the meeting disbanded. The plan could work. But would it? There was one way in which the plan could prevail, but a thousand ways with which it could fall to wrack and ruin. The Armenian could be a gift from God – or a tool of Satan. The bishop had helped to patch-up the council again, but Adhemar knew the delicate stitching could fall apart at the seams at any juncture. All it would take was one misplaced word. Tensions were swelling, like the belly of a corpse left out in the sun, between Raymond and Bohemond. Bohemond could take the city, but then Raymond might endeavour to take it off his rival. Too much Christian blood had been spilled during this campaign already, but not by Christian hands. That might soon change, Adhemar lamented.

The dry heat sapped his strength and spirit. As much as the bishop preached that there was a distinct separation between the body and soul, he wasn't now so sure. But only faith can be shared. Never doubts. His head hurt, as if he were wearing a crown of thorns. Adhemar decided to distract himself by conducting his daily visit of the pilgrims' camp. Unfortunately, the experience did little to elevate his mood, although he forced himself to put on a brave, kind expression. It was his job to give people hope, faith – even when he felt devoid of those virtues himself.

"Sometimes it will feel that you are more of an actor, than a man of God," Urban had explained, before setting off on the campaign. "You must be an inspiration to your flock, especially when you feel uninspired yourself, my friend. The princes and pilgrims will need you to be a rock. If gold should rust, what will lead do?"

Gormless, god-fearing and goodly expressions greeted him as he walked through the dilapidated camp. He often swung a hand in front of his face to shoo away the throngs of insects. Many pilgrims he had encountered in the camp before approached him. Some courted him for a blessing, whilst clutching the hem of his robes. Adhemar regretted that his words could only provide consolation, as opposed to sustenance. Others asked him questions which he couldn't answer. Or if he did know the answer, it would be best if he didn't share his grim thoughts. When was the Emperor – and his army – coming? When would the next fleet of ships, laden with supplies, from Cyprus be arriving? Some revealed how they were fasting, in honour of God – but in truth they were starving. Some resembled walking skeletons. Skin stretched over protruding bones. Tears bled into sweat on moist, radish coloured cheeks. Emaciated children lay curled-up on the ground in what shade they could find, like dogs, to avoid the infernal sun.

Antioch loomed in the background. The bishop permitted himself an indulgent prayer that, after the assault, the crusader banners would be hanging over the city. Adhemar immediately cringed however – because for that to happen, scores of Antiochenes would be slaughtered. The banners would be bloodstained. How Christian could the crusaders claim to be after the campaign was over?

If they survived the ordeal.

As was his habit Adhemar visited Jean Mauger and his family in the camp. Their tent was housed on a slight slope. After hearing a sermon from his local bishop, calling for all men to take the cross, the former soldier turned fisherman decided to sell his boat and business. His wife and four children would accompany him. Jean wanted to see Jerusalem – and the Holy of Holies. God was calling him. Did he believe that God had called two of his children home, before they even reached the fringe of the Byzantine Empire? Yet Jean remained undaunted. There would be no turning back. Adhemar admired the humble Frank. He never complained or took his frustrations and privations out on his companions. Jean remained devoted to his wife - and doted on his children. The scarred and gnarled-faced soldier was unfailingly courteous and kind. Such was his size, strength and faith that many in the camp nicknamed him "Sampson". Sometimes Adhemar thought his congregant might be a simpleton. Despite all he had endured, the pilgrim believed in God and goodness. Jean saw the best in people and still naively believed he would see Jerusalem.

Godfrey of Bouillon was waiting for the bishop when he returned. Ostensibly the soldier desired for Adhemar to hear his confession, shrive his soul, before the assault tomorrow. The Christian prince was not beyond politicking too though. Godfrey, subtly or otherwise, petitioned Adhemar to nominate him as the steward of Jerusalem should they eventually capture the Holy City.

"If you call upon me, I will do my duty," Godfrey argued, placing his palm on the cross sewn into his tabard, just below his left shoulder, as he spoke.

Adhemar politely replied that he would give due consideration to his petition. Not only did he force a smile, but the clergyman forced his eyes open, lest he fall asleep. His bed called out to him, like the voice of God.

"I should inform you – albeit it will come as no great surprise to you I imagine - that I have received a number of other petitions, selflessly offering to take stewardship of Jerusalem. But you will appreciate how I cannot put the cart before the horse. Our thoughts must be focussed on Antioch, before they can turn towards the Holy City… Please forgive me Godfrey. It is now time for my daily prayers."

The prince had barely left the tent when Adhemar dismissed his attendant and took to his bed, curling up like the children he observed earlier. Even when asleep however the bishop scarce seemed at peace.

Adhemar's clerk, Rainald, passed on several messages when his master woke. Most concerned a variety of princes and clergymen inviting the bishop to dinner. A last supper, Adhemar wryly thought.

"You are popular this evening," Rainald remarked.

"I know. Alas. I must make a note to pray for the contrary. It seems everyone wants a piece of me. I'm not sure there's enough to go around. I do not quite possess the energy to be flattered, supplicated or interrogated throughout the night."

Adhemar wondered whether he had tried to court his superiors to further his career. Had he been fawning towards the likes of Urban and Raymond in the name of ambition? He couldn't discount it. Churchmen could be even more ruthless than soldiers or politicians, when pursuing promotion. No doubt people believed that they could manipulate him, as Adhemar believed he could charm Urban and Raymond. The nobleman tried his best to remain uncorrupted over the years. Adhemar's private wealth meant he was immune to bribes. The bishop had never been tempted by women, or young men, like many of his colleagues. Yet he couldn't claim to be wholly free from pride and vanity. Had Urban not persuaded him to take the cross due to the prize of him writing his place in history? He had claimed to work for the glory of God. But had he not done so for the glory of his own name? Had he not sinned?

Adhemar instructed Rainald to politely refuse the array of invitations. Instead, the bishop decided to ask Edward to his tent to share a jug of wine. The soldier would not spend the evening flattering him, or bidding for a remission of his sins. The thought of Edward trying to do so amused the bishop.

As Rainald was about to take his leave Adhemar realised that he could tell his clerk to launder his ceremonial robes, in anticipation of the Emperor's arrival or his staff could attend to his armour and weaponry. There wasn't time for both in the morning. He chose the latter option.

The two friends worked their way through a simple meal of warm flat bread, soft cheese and salted pork. Adhemar felt queasy and handed over his plate to Edward, who needed the extra sustenance to keep up his strength. The soldier would have a long day, or night, tomorrow.

"What did you think about the meeting earlier today?" the bishop asked, wishing to glean a different perspective on events.

"If we spent as much time and cunning fighting against the enemy than we do each other then we would be in Jerusalem already, I warrant," the Englishman replied, before fishing a piece of pork out from in between his teeth and popping it back into his mouth.

"Do you believe Bohemond's plan will work?"

"It will have to. It's the only plan we have, unless a herd of winged horses arrive and we're able to fly over the walls. If there's one thing that you can have faith in, it's that Bohemond likes to win. And he's doubly determined. Taking the city will mean victory over both the Turks and Raymond. The key will be opening the gates. The enemy won't be able to then stem the tide. We'll swallow the bastards up like a leviathan. But be careful what you wish for. I've seen a city sacked before. It's been more than six months of us snarling outside the walls. Six months of misery. Six months of rage. Mercy will be in shorter supply than wine. As much as you may be tempted to try and oversee or intervene in relation to the assault I would caution you in standing in between a soldier and his loot," Edward remarked, internally shuddering as he imagined the scenes to come – scenes he had witnessed during previous sackings. He could still hear the ripping of dresses, the crackle of flames as homes were torched, the sluicing sound as blades scythed through flesh and the wailing screams of women and children, before being grimly silenced.

"We men are wretched things," Homer said, echoing the soldier's thoughts. Sighing. "There are some truths which even pre-date the Bible."

As the evening wore on Adhemar noticed that something was troubling his friend. The Englishman was only drinking half as much as usual (which was still twice as much as most men). The bishop naturally considered that Edward could be being haunted by the shadow of death hanging over him. Bohemond would doubtless volunteer him to take part in the initial force to enter the city and open the gates. Notwithstanding the issue of Firuz potentially betraying the crusaders, if the besiegers spotted the enemy then they would overwhelm them. Corner them. Torture them. Butcher them. Adhemar also suspected that his friend's thoughts were turning towards Emma. Finally, he had something, or someone, to fight for. The bishop had observed the way he looked at the woman – and was amused by the tough soldier being vulnerable and enamoured. He joked to his companion that he may even feel compelled to compose some love poetry. Adhemar also asked if the Englishman ever felt like getting married.

"I thought about it, once," Edward had replied. "But the thought passed, like a bout of the shits."

Flames licked the air, writhing like lissom, limber dancers. Emma made sure to place a couple of braziers just outside and inside the tent. The warm, perfumed air was inviting. Enticing.

But it wasn't solely due to the hot air that Thomas stood, with his face flushed. Blushing. Part of him wanted to avert his gaze. But not enough of him, it seemed, as he continued to snatch glimpses of flesh, glowing in the candlelight, through slits in dresses and plunging necklines. In some instances, there was an absence of any neckline. Thomas' eyes bulged. He stopped gawping upon hearing the booming laughter of Owen inside, still happily spending his winnings from his wager.

Thomas had come to the tent to seek out Edward. He wanted to discuss a plan with his friend to find and save Yeva, after infiltrating the city. Thomas declined an invitation to enter and look for his countryman. It would have been tantamount to a sin. Instead, he patiently waited outside as an attendant searched for Edward. Thomas found himself musing on the figure of Yeva, again. He pictured her with glossy black hair and smooth, olive skin. A heart-shaped face. She was beautiful – but also virginal. He pictured scenes of him teaching her English – and she would ask him about his homeland. Her husband was conveniently absent. Thomas' heart swelled when he thought of the young woman. Of saving her, as if he were a knight errant. It was his fate, destiny, to protect her. God willed it. The student had even composed some verses, in his head, in honour of his muse. He found himself admiring her, even though he didn't know her – and Yeva didn't even know he existed.

Herleva was usually attentive and responsive to her customers. She made a conscious effort to remember their names and feign interest in their lives (especially married men, who were apt to feign guilt). She knew how to play a part and could tantalise different types of customer like a harpist plucking strings. But she barely noticed as a bushy-bearded knight put his hand between her legs and wetly nuzzled her neck. He was aroused enough for the both of them. Her plan would be to extract a further payment and finish him off quickly. She would then have a cup of wine with Emma and move on to her next client.

The girl was distracted, from seeing Thomas outside through the crowd of people. Initially she thought he might finally succumb to temptation and enter. If he did so she would give her current customer his money back and rush over to him, before any of the girls pounced on him. Herleva didn't know whether to be upset with Thomas or not when he declined to enter the tent. The den of iniquity, as the Christian once labelled it. She realised that he was probably looking for Edward. Thomas was unlike others, who tarried outside the brothel and peered inside, unable to afford to enter. They would ogle the girls from afar. Sometimes they even touched themselves, their eyes glazed over with unfiltered desire. She remembered one man who stood outside for so long, in the rain, that he began to sink into the mud.

Herleva stared at the Englishman with a blithe fondness. He looked so innocent, like he was in a world of his own. She wondered what he was thinking about. She imagined he might even be thinking about her. The uneducated whore remembered their last conversation. Thomas had offered to teach her to read and write.

"I could only pay you back in one way," she had replied, half-teasing the virginal Christian.

Thomas crimsoned, from root to tip.

"You wouldn't have to pay me. A good deed is its own reward."

If anyone else would have uttered the line they would have sounded pompous. But Thomas was somehow incapable of being insincere.

Herleva had countless admirers, but few true friends. Her sense of fondness faded, to be replaced by twinges of sadness. She wanted to be closer to Thomas. She liked him. She envied his faith. He was innocent enough for the both of them. On more than one occasion she fancied what it might be like to be married to him. Thomas would never cheat on her or abuse her. When Herleva first started in her profession she dreamed of a nobleman or knight falling in love with her, whisking her away to live in a castle and showering her with silk dresses and gifts. But princes and knights were not what they seemed. They were fool's gold. Thomas was something better – a good man, the kind of man who would make a good husband and father. Herleva had always been brazen and unapologetic about her profession – but she dared to dream about what life would be like in the Englishman's homeland, far away from the damned crusade and her past life. He represented a new chapter in her life. Thomas made her want to be a better person, to be good enough for him.

The bearded soldier let out a guttural hum or groan of pleasure. It had been an age since his grimy fingers had pawed such soft skin. He drank in her perfume. Herleva whispered a term of endearment into his wiry-haired ear, but then rolled her eyes afterwards. She would close her eyes and imagine being with Thomas when she was in bed with him.

"Do you want to come out back? I want to be with you," the Norman said, letting out a slight whistling noise through his bushy nostrils after he spoke.

"I'm all yours, darling, for as long as you want me," she replied, before standing up. The whore planted a kiss on his salivating mouth, avoiding wincing – or retching – and led him away. "Let me tell you about some of my extras. I like you. I can give you a discount."

She glanced back one last time at the Englishman, through the lascivious crowd, before disappearing with her customer. Herleva admired him, but it was as though she didn't exist.

"Have I got you drunk enough yet for you to submit to me hearing your confession, Edward?" Adhemar asked, only half-jokingly. The bishop was conscious of avoiding saying his "last" confession.

"You'll never get me that drunk, although I wouldn't want to dissuade you from trying," the knight replied, raising his cup in a mock toast. "We also both need our sleep. I'm concerned that I'd keep you up all night if I confessed my sins. But rather than worry about my soul, or a lack of one, we need to plan for the worse, in relation to yours. God knows what will happen over the next few days, if indeed God even cares. But I'd feel comfortable knowing that you will be safe. You have been our steadfast guide. We probably would not have reached this far without you, Adhemar. You have kept a pack of wolves together. As much as they may have howled and snarled it is due to your leadership that they haven't turned on each other in earnest. Each of those preening princes owe you – so if any of them offer you safe passage back home you should accept. I'd also advise you to say yes to more than one offer, as who knows which of them will be alive to fulfil their promise. The Turks will see you as a prize worth seeking out and capturing, to be ransomed," Edward argued, conscious of avoiding saying how it was more likely their foes would torture and kill the priest.

12.

The army, consisting of men-at-arms and knights, had massed and commenced to depart. Bohemond made sure that only a few people knew about his grand plan. The fewer the better. He couldn't afford for anyone inside the city to know his intentions. The plan could only work if Siyan was convinced by their ruse.

The confusion and crestfallen expressions on the faces of his soldiers were genuine. Mossy beards seemed more scraggly than usual. Figures were as thin and pale as silver birch trees. Misery infected their beings, as surely as crosses were worn on shoulders. The majority of the crusaders believed they were retreating. They trundled, instead of marched. Dragging their feet. Dust scuffed up as they slowly advanced towards the mountain passes. Their heads were bowed, like chastened children. Their stomachs grumbled. Water couldn't wash away the bitter taste of defeat. Was God testing or punishing them? Or was the shame and agony a form of purgatory, before reaching Jerusalem? Sweat trickled down wan features, caked with dust and sand. Armour chinked. Joints ached. The sweltering heat rubbed salt into the wound, as did the taunts and cheers from the walls of the city. Some fainted.

Let them jeer, Bohemond thought to himself.

I'll soon wipe the smile off their faces. With my mace.

The military column lumbered, undulating, like a world-weary serpent. Fangless. Many of the soldiers could barely remember the moment they committed themselves (or Bohemond committed them) to the campaign. They had been captivated by the promise of riches and the remission of sins. Trying to remember life in Italy was like trying to remember the details of a disintegrating dream. Soldiering across Europe could be hard and bloody. But the crusade was tantamount to suicide. Saints and martyrs had suffered less.

Raymond stood on the balcony, outside his bedchamber, and watched the procession of soldiers tamp away. His features and heart were conflicted. He duly wanted the army to succeed – but for the commander leading the assault to fail. To die in battle. He wondered if it would be suitable to pray to God for the Almighty to alter the course of a stray arrow and lodge it in his rival's breast.

The count wasn't the only figure to stop and stare at the departing force. Adhemar gazed into the distance, as if he were trying to peer into the future. Divining it. The bishop could not claim to be a prophet or visionary. He thought how he was unlike Peter the Hermit. Thank God. Many of the men appeared doom-laden when they were issued with their orders earlier, to retreat. But the poor souls would soon realise that they were gifting everyone hope. Salvation. Bohemond was adamant that the army should initially be kept in the dark. Untrustworthy people are seldom given to trusting others, Adhemar judged. The clergyman watched as the final combatant passed out of view. He wished he could find out all the names in the army and issue a prayer for each one. Instead he uttered a solitary word as an all-encompassing benediction.

"Godspeed."

Emma also observed the column snake towards the mountain passes, cursing herself for having missed Edward. For not saying goodbye properly – and letting him know how she felt about him. She had sensed that something had been wrong yesterday, after Edward met with Bohemond. The knight explained that a sizeable portion of the army was departing, to form a giant foraging party. But Emma was a woman attuned to knowing when a man was lying. She'd had plenty of practice over the years. Usually it was when a man moved his lips. Yet

Edward had been largely honest with her. It was partly why she was so attracted to him.

Was this the first stage of a retreat? Or were they finally advancing towards Jerusalem? Emma had more questions than answers, unfortunately. Edward had promised that he would return:

"Sooner than you might think. If nothing else I'll be back because I'll miss my new horse too much," he said with a half-smile.

Emma stood beside Herleva. At best wistful, at worst mournful. Tears moistened her lugubrious eyes. She half-smiled, as she pictured the Englishman, and clasped the hand of her friend, not quite knowing the reason why.

Edward walked on, having decided to leave the mount Adhemar had lent him back at the camp. For Emma. He had missed her last night and earlier in the morning. She was well-versed in climbing in and out of bed without waking her sleeping partner. All that remained of her presence was the lingering scent of her perfume on the bedsheet. Edward had prepared a short speech for Emma, but he didn't get the chance to air it. The soldier was not one for sentiment or flowery words, but he wanted to ask Emma if she would like to come back to England with him. He had some savings and planned to buy a cottage. He had drawn his sword enough. Too much. An old friend, a former sell-sword, had offered to sell him a share in his tavern. He wanted to settle and a place to call home. The word "home" had caused Edward disquiet before, as he remembered his childhood and what the company of Normans – the pack of wolves – had done to his village. But with Emma he was willing to make a home again, instead of just forgetting about his old one. Or if she invited him back to Taranto, he would accept. He wanted to tell Emma that he had woken up to lots of different women in the past, but in the future Edward only wanted to wake up to one for his remaining years in the world. The Englishman was a little fearful of scaring Emma away, however. She had revealed how several men had offered to marry her before. "They wanted me, partly because they didn't want anyone else to have me," the whore confessed. "They wanted to yoke me, like a prize bull. But I ran away, faster than a thoroughbred horse."

The Englishman yearned to say so much, to drink in her smile and hear her laughter for at least one last time. Instead, Edward had said nothing. It was another reason why he needed to see her again. For the first time, in a long time, the soldier put together a semblance of a prayer.

I know we haven't spoken in an age – and I've got more sins to atone for than a relic-selling priest or inbred nobleman – but I'm not petitioning you for me. I just want you to keep her safe. She's worth ten, or a hundred, of me. Should I say an Our Father? I'll be in your debt. How should I pay you back? I promise not to take your name in vain, for at least a month. If you prove that you can be merciful and benevolent – then I'll prove myself to you in return.

Thomas made his way along the column, his eyes darting about like a bee seeking honey, as he looked to locate Edward. Time was running out to form a plan to save Yeva. He barely slept during the night, as he played out various scenarios of meeting the young woman. When he did sleep though, he dreamed of her. Or someone he believed was her. Was God showing him a vision? A sign?

As much as Thomas' inward eye dwelled on the dusky, exotic beauty of Yeva, the Englishman couldn't help but note the drear, emaciated figures in front of him. A few of the soldiers, from Bohemond's company, Thomas knew. Gaston. The infantryman's mouth was downturned, in an inverted V-shape.

The man-at-arms was clutching a small vial of holy water, which hung around his neck. He believed the water made him invulnerable in battle. Next to him was Walter, a former tanner. His scalp shone in the late afternoon sun, from where the soldier rubbed vinegar and honey into his skin – due to an apothecary recommending the remedy as a cure for his baldness. Walter appeared even more grief-stricken than usual. The Italian had travelled east with his three brothers. He was the last one remaining. The soldiers had died six months apart, throughout the pilgrimage. With each death Walter had grown more embittered. Each death had been like the swing of an axe, Thomas mused, hacking away at his faith and good nature. And the tree was on the cusp of finally falling. The innkeeper's son, who was fond of singing and brewing his own ale, was the shadow of the man he once was. His roseate cheeks had hollowed out. He no longer attended mass. His default expression was a choleric scowl.

Thomas was at one point tempted to console some of the soldiers by confiding in them. Their ignominious retreat was merely a ruse. But Bohemond had threatened his inner circle with all manner of punishments should they become loose-lipped.

His thighs burned. Beads of sweat wended their way across his downy cheeks. But Thomas was a man possessed. He needed to find his countryman before it grew too dark and they doubled-back towards the city. He had gulped in fear, more than once, at the prospect of trying to find Yeva without Edward's help. But not even Charlemagne or Caesar could sway him from his duty. He believed it was fate, that he would save the woman. And so he continued to work his way along the bedraggled line, like a man possessed or a beggar scrabbling around for a few small coins buried in the mud.

Alexios Komnenos didn't need to hear too much to know that he had heard enough. He would abandon the crusaders to their fate, if they hadn't already met their demise.

Stephen of Blois stood before him. His features were drawn, as if they had been stretched out on a rack. He was anxious. Anxious to be on his way, back to Normandy. to know if he would receive a reward from the Emperor, to not be thought a coward, no better than the lowliest deserter. Timidity and dishonour eked out of the pores of his skin like sweat, Tatikios mused, as he looked on. Even before the campaign commenced in earnest, the Byzantine general had scant affection or admiration for the Norman prince. He was thin-bloodied. One would always find him at the rear of a cavalry charge. Alexios had employed one of his spies to intercept his correspondence with his wife, Adela, when the Norman stayed as his guest in Constantinople. She dominated him. He was a whipped cur. "She is the husband and he is the wife," Tatikios had joked at the time.

The prince had encountered a Byzantine scout during his trek to Alexandretta - and requested to seek an audience with the Emperor. He reported that the campaign was lost. Desertions, disease and starvation were rife within the legion. Antioch was no closer to surrendering. Kerbogha's army was three times the strength of the western forces. Better armed. Better provisioned. Fresher. If the pilgrims remained, they would be attacked. If attacked, defeated.

Alexios had hoped to arrive at Antioch with the crusaders and Turks having half mauled each other – and he would be in a position of strength to snatch the city away from both of them. But it wasn't now worth advancing. His army would return to Constantinople. Consolidate. As deplorable as Stephen of Blois' cowardice was, the Emperor would have deserted the doomed cause too in his position. Although he was fond of a few of the westerners, most notably Adhemar, he despised the pilgrims as a tribe. As a race they were vulgar, crapulent and brutish – and that was just their ruling class. The Emperor recalled his daughter's judgement about the Normans. "They are like gangrene, for gangrene, once established in a body, never rests until it has invaded and corrupted the whole of it." Alexios did not wish to fall out with Urban, however, as he may need the pope's assistance again. Allies were better than enemies. He may be persuasive enough, or Urban may be gullible enough, to call for another crusade. Alexios would spare a thought for the doomed pilgrims and pray for them, although he would also offer up a prayer of thanks to Kerbogha for removing the irritant of Bohemond. The more his old enemy suffered in death, the better, he unchristianly thought. If they decapitated the infidel, he would bid to purchase the head as a trophy.

The Byzantine Emperor was reclined on a large sofa. The Norman bowed his head slightly, awaiting his response. His eyes flitted about him, taking in the various attendants standing just outside the tent, ready to be called upon. To serve. There was a barber, cupbearer, surgeon, courtesans, a cook and even perfumer. A couple of brawny slaves stood either side of the tent and gently waved fans over the head of their master. A quartet of Varangians stood pillar-like at each corner of the canopy. Red-haired. Freckled. Were they English? The famed, formidable soldiers looked like they wouldn't piss on the Norman if he was on fire. The attendants were ready to unleash themselves and attend to their emperor's every whim. He rewarded loyalty and exemplary service - but had few qualms about punishing anyone who displeased him.

Alexios smoothed down his already oiled hair and straightened the sapphire ring on his middle finger. He paused before replying, before passing judgement. It often amused him to keep people waiting. He fought off the temptation to yawn.

"We shall pray for your companions," the Emperor piously stated, briefly creasing his fine features in a show of sympathy. But Alexios had little intention of offering any other form of assistance to his allies to support the war effort. The campaign was over. Constantinople would provision and allow sanctuary for any retreating crusaders, on the condition that they moved on quickly. One should never reward failure.

Abrasive clouds scoured the sky in the distance. Edward imagined that the soldiers would welcome the rain. The fiercer the storm the better. They would raise their leathery faces to the heavens. Catch the water in their helmets. Lick their lips. They could even believe, for a few moments, that the rain might wash their sins away.

Perhaps some of the soldiers were looking forward to marching into the tempest. Unfortunately, they would soon be turning back to advance into a different type of storm. The storm of war. And so they went on. Edward wondered which would wear thin first, the soles of his boots or his patience.

Thomas had finally caught up with him – and acted like a fly in his ear. Pleading with him. Pestering him. The scribe could talk for England – and every other country represented in the campaign, Edward mused. He talked and gesticulated incessantly, like a religious zealot.

"I am willing to defer to you, as to how we should proceed to find and save Yeva once we have entered the city. I have memorised a map of the area and more than one route from the walls to the house."

"You shouldn't be getting your hopes up. The lass may even have perished in the past month."

"No! I know that she's still alive. And I know that we will save her. God wills it," Thomas shot back, frantically. His voice suddenly became shriller. The scrawny youth also gripped the knight's arm as he spoke, and for once Edward considered that his friend might be stronger than he looked. He also considered that Thomas was obsessing over the girl. The holy fool was turning into a love-struck poet. The world-weary knight was tempted to tell the green youth how love, like life, would chew him up and spit him out.

"Sometimes things do not always work out how we would like," Edward cautioned. Sometimes spirits needed dampening. The soldier hoped that the trauma of battle would curtail his desire to rescue the girl.

"I have faith that we will find her. I also have faith in you, Edward."

"People have been foolish enough to have faith in me before. I don't have much faith in me, lad, so I'm not sure why you should," Edward replied, a voice baked in regrets and soaked in wine.

"You gave your word to Varhan though."

"It was just a word. Once said, it disappeared into the ether. No one else heard it."

"God did."

"I pity God then, if he has nothing worthier to do than eavesdrop on my conversations," Edward cuttingly remarked.

Thomas, for once, was silent. Edward had hoped earlier that his companion would cease speaking. But be careful what you wish for. The youth appeared hurt – worrying that the knight would break his promise and blood would be on their hands. For a moment the adolescent appeared like he might even cry. Edward felt a pang of guilt, as if someone had plunged a small blade in his back during a tavern brawl. The soldier told himself that he shouldn't feel guilty. He told himself that, unless he broke his promise to Varhan, both he and Thomas would be killed on the streets of Antioch. Trying to "rescue a virtuous maiden," as the would-be knight had naively explained it.

But it wasn't just Thomas' voice Edward heard in his head as night began to fall. Again, he heard his mother's words - touching what little remained of his hobbled heart.

"You should always keep a promise."

"Why?"

"Because God is watching you."

13.

Darkness was their friend. The wind was also blustery, muffling out the noise they made. God was on their side. Sixty or so knights moved forward towards the steep walls of Antioch and the Tower of Two Sisters. Carefully. Stealthily. Curses were whispered beneath breaths every time a rock was kicked out of place or a scabbard scraped against the ground. Any mail or metal was covered-up or smeared with mud so there was no danger of it being caught in any light.

It appeared that the ramparts above them were free of watchers. So far, so good. Firuz has either dismissed the men from that part of the wall – or the ruse had worked and the Antiochenes were elsewhere, celebrating their victory over the westerners.

Bohemond led the elite troops. Many were from noble families. Many were devout Christians. More than one had studied to serve in the church. Some composed poetry. But most were cold-bloodied killers. Killing came as easily as breathing to the soldiers. More than chivalric knights, they were butchers. Thank God, Bohemond thought. Most wouldn't hesitate to slice open a woman or child's throat, if they stood in the way of the company opening the gates. Their blood would be up, but they would keep a clear head too. The mission was everything.

Candles illuminated a window, glimmering in the darkness, guiding them in. Bohemond was reminded of an evening in his youth. The lusty scion of Robert Guiscard had arranged a late-night assignation with a nobleman's daughter. She had placed candles in her bedroom window, as a signal that it was safe for Bohemond to climb up to her chamber. Once inside her room he suspected that the girl was not as virginal as she claimed to be. A month later, after Bohemond begun to court another mistress, the nobleman's daughter confessed to being with child. His response was to curse the girl for being stupid – and a whore. He accused her of trying to trap him into marrying her – and that he wasn't the father. He would disown her and the child. Bohemond's sigh of relief could be heard throughout Taranto however when he learned that the girl lost the baby.

The prize behind the window now was greater than any young woman, virginal or otherwise. Bohemond decided that others could be first to claim the prize and glory of entering the city, however. He would no longer lead his force of knights, who were charged with scaling the walls and opening the gates. Partly he wanted to command the bulk of his troops, in order secure the citadel. But partly he was scared, although he would never openly confess to such weakness. His soldiers were about to cross the Rubicon. Once inside the walls, should Siyan attack, they would be cornered. Slaughtered. The Army of God needed Bohemond alive, he conveniently told himself. The coming hour could decide the fate of the entire campaign. He could not enjoy the spoils of victory if he was dead.

Bohemond was understandably not the only soul to be frightened. Sixty soldiers were about to enter a city garrisoned with five thousand, who would take great pleasure in flaying and murdering them. Their heads would be removed from their mutilated bodies and tossed over the wall the next morning, like rotten vegetables, if they were captured. Even in the inky darkness Bohemond witnessed the trepidation, or barely suppressed terror, in the faces of some of his men. Even the bravest of combatants were not immune to fear. It poured through the world like a chill wind. Teeth chattered. Crosses were clutched. The prince thought it apt to say a few words, to put some steel into his men, as they observed the rope being lowered from the window.

So far, so good.

"Go on, strong in heart and fortunate in your comrades, and scale the ladder into Antioch, for by God's will we shall have it in our possession in a trice... Songs will be sung about your courage and deeds tonight. God will reward you in Heaven and I will reward you in this life. Let no sword be unstained with the infidel's blood. The enemy has jeered at us, resisted us, for the last time. The city will be ours. God wills it."

Although the men didn't understandably cheer, their sinews stiffened.

The ladder was brought up.

Whether suffering from the cold, or fear, Hugh's hands trembled as he attached the rope to the siege ladder.

The ladder was pulled up and fixed into position.

Fulk of Chartres had approached his prince beforehand and volunteered to be the first to scale the walls. The stolidly built knight owned a flat, hard face – which only ever softened, slightly, after several measures of wine. Fulk was not given to frivolity. Bohemond once joked to Edward that he had only ever seen the stoical soldier smile three times:

"The first was when he killed a man in battle, the second was when he was told he would be exempted from paying tax for the year and the last time was when he heard the news that his mother-in-law had died."

Fulk could sometimes be as stubborn as a mule, but he could fight like a lion. He ground his teeth in grim determination as he climbed. The pilgrim was keen to avenge the deaths of fellow Christians who had fallen throughout the siege.

Next to put a foot on a rung of the ladder, after fraternally clasping the hand of his commander and exchanging some words of encouragement, was Hugh. He prayed beneath his breath. The closer a soldier is to death, the closer he gets to God.

Next up was Edward. His heart was throbbing, like a bee sting. His expression wasn't etched in fear, but the Englishman could have just been burying his feelings, as deep as a grave, like usual. His sigh got lost in the soughing wind. Before climbing, the soldier turned to Thomas, whose face was as pale as the anaemic moon. The scribe took a step back from the ladder - but looked like he wanted to take a hundred more. His bottom lip was quivering. Bohemond's words seemed to have instilled fear rather than fearlessness in his heart.

"Follow me up, lad. Every journey starts with a first step. You won't be able to save your Yeva this side of the walls," Edward said, hoping that the girl could inspire him, if Bohemond had failed to do so. The knight wiped his sweaty palms one last time and clasped the ladder, offering up the semblance of a prayer too as he did so.

Let her live. Even if I have to die.

They climbed the ladder. It bowed but didn't break – like the courage of the men who ascended. Into the belly of the beast. Thomas' foot slipped on a rung a couple of times and he hugged the ladder for dear life – wrapping his arms around it like the way he used to embrace not a woman, but his Bible and other tomes. Owen offered words of encouragement or censure, as he followed the youth up the walls.

Firuz tapped his foot and pulled and twirled his beard. He licked his chapped lips and straightened the fringe of his increasingly greying hair. His build was slight – spindly, like a sapling in winter. The Armenian had aged more in the past two months than he had in the previous two years. Tonight would be the making of him – or end him. Firuz told himself again that he was doing the right thing - and reminded himself of Yaghi Siyan's slight against him. He envisioned confronting Siyan after the city had been taken from him – and before the tyrant faced execution. Firuz was glad that Bohemond agreed he would spare civilians and only allow soldiers to perish – and only if they resisted. But both men knew they were lying to each other and themselves. They would have blood on their hands. Firuz raked his fingernails down his neck once more, as his nervous rash flared up again.

"I am Firuz," the Armenian said, gulping as he did so. His voice was strained, as if someone had recently tried to strangle him. "We have so few Franks. Where is Bohemond?"

Edward, Owen, Hugh, Thomas and Fulk of Chartres stood before him. Thomas thought the armourer would be burlier. Or that the traitor would possess sharper, shadier features. His bulbous eyes were framed within feminine lashes. A couple of watchmen flanked Firuz, who appeared equally nervous. Perhaps they felt uneasy, guilty, about their treachery. Or perhaps they were worried that the Franks might slay them, or that Firuz might not pay the bribe he promised them.

The Armenian spoke Greek. Thomas translated.

"We have enough Franks," Fulk replied, bluntly. Upbraiding. Slightly offended. The Christian believed himself superior to the infidel. "Bohemond will be leading our forces when we open the gates. We are bringing up your next instalment of gold, to answer his next question."

Firuz proceeded to hastily explain how he had dismissed his company from their duties this evening, but that the adjacent watchtowers were still manned.

"There are only two men in each of the towers. Others are out celebrating. I have checked. They must be prevented from alerting others. They have a bell and lantern, which serve as a warning system," the Armenian advised.

Hugh and Edward discussed how they would need to take the towers by guile rather than force. They would need to kill rather than wound. The two knights would take personal responsibility for leading the attacks on the nearby watchtowers. Edward would pair up with Owen, Hugh would recruit Fulk.

The room began to fill out with the western knights as they clambered through the window, either shaken by the climb or the prospect of the formidable fight ahead. Dust marks on the floor indicated how Firuz had emptied the chamber of furniture, to accommodate the swelling numbers of his allies.

As the armourer took himself away into a corner, opening-up his chest of gold and counting his fee, Edward and Owen peeled off out of the room and walked up the stairs – to the battlements. The cold wind swirled and ululated, like a wolf. A few campfires pockmarked the plains, as stars pockmarked the night sky.

"Surprise will be on our side," the Englishman said encouragingly, his breath misting up in front of his face.

"Aye, and surprise is a cheaper ally it seems than the Armenian downstairs," the Welshman replied, as he drew a shaft from his cloth arrow bag, which hung over his shoulder, next to his waist.

It wouldn't be too long until dawn, as opposed to darkness, would be their friend, Edward considered. Providing visibility to view the houses worth looting, the enemy worth slaying and the women worth tupping.

But at the moment darkness was still their friend – as the two crusaders walked, with the archer concealed behind the knight, along the ramparts towards the watchtower. Edward walked slowly, nonchalantly, as he closed in on the two Antiochenes standing at the entrance to the guard tower. It was too dark - and he was too far away - for the guards to notice that it was a western face coming towards them. They were also blind to the archer advancing behind the figure. Owen had already nocked his arrow. He couldn't afford to miss.

Kill, don't wound.

It was almost time, Edward judged. They were close enough for the enemy to provide a sufficiently large target, but not so close where the guards might notice something amiss. The Englishman unassumingly moved his hand around his back, reaching for a dagger concealed there. As to their plan he launched his blade at the enemy on the right, as Owen appeared out behind him, like a thief or avenging angel. Pull. Loose. The recently sharpened arrowhead pierced through the guard's leather jerkin – and burst his heart - as if it were made of gossamer. He was dead, not wounded. Thankfully the missile forced the guard backwards, as opposed to him staggering sideways and falling down from the battlements, onto the street below.

Edward's knife hit its mark too. The target was the Turk's upper chest – or unprotected throat. Blood flooded the guard's lungs and drowned out any screams. As soon as the knight launched his dagger however he was rushing towards the guard, whilst drawing a second blade, which hung from the front of his belt. No sooner had his opponent hit the ground than the knight was upon him, like a lion placing a paw on its prey's flank and ripping open its neck. The guard only had time to offer up an expression of shock and terror, before Edward covered his mouth and slit his throat, hacking through his windpipe as if he were carving an overcooked piece of steak.

So far, so good.

14.

Shortly after Edward and Owen returned downstairs, Hugh and Fulk came back, having similarly completed their mission. Edward wasn't the only soldier in the room who was taken aback by Fulk's gruesome visage. His cheeks, mouth and chin glistened with blood and even tiny pieces of bone – like grains of rice in a stew. The Norman's wolfish grin could still be discerned beneath the red mask. Edward mused how he could now inform Bohemond that there was another instance of Fulk smiling. If he lived to tell the tale. The chronicles would no doubt portray Fulk as a chivalric knight, who had fought bravely and honourably to capture the watchtower. Everything was all so fucking laughable for the Englishman.

The room hummed with the sound of whispered conversations and prayers. Hugh sensed that he wasn't the only one whose skin was prickling with cold and apprehension. As Bohemond advised, the knight offered up a few words to focus their minds:

"Our brothers are waiting for us on the other side of the gates. Let us open the doors and welcome them in. This night may be blacker than a Moor's arse, but the day is always darkest before the dawn. Come the morning our banners will hang over these walls. God wills it!"

Again, the knights suppressed any urge to cheer, keeping a lid of their bubbling pot. But their hearts were hardened - and gauntlets gripped pommels – as Hugh led the company out of the chamber. To give battle.

As Thomas, waiting at the rear of the group, was about to set-off as well he was approached by Edward. The knight placed a hand on the youth's shoulder, either as a gesture of fraternity or to prevent him from moving.

"I want you to remain here, lad, where it's safe. You're here to act as a translator. But the time for talking is over. It's about deeds, not words," Edward argued.

"But what about our mission to save Yeva?"

"I promise to come back once we have opened the gate," the knight replied, with little conviction.

Thomas was going to assert that he wanted to see deeds, not words.

Edward strode out of the room, telling himself that he couldn't afford to be distracted from his task. His duty was towards Bohemond rather than God. Yet he was torn, like a traveller coming to a fork in the road. God was becoming a cancer, eating away at his selfishness. If he kept his word, honour, and saved Yeva - would God then protect Emma? Even when he considered that he was starting to behave like a holy fool, he couldn't prevent himself from scratching the itch. Should the knight somehow survive the battle to open the gates, should he then risk everything again to save the girl? She might not even be at home by the time he got there. God and Thomas might never forgive him if he broke his promise, however. Edward felt damned if he did – and damned if he didn't – in relation to saving Varhan's niece.

The knights marched along a street, which ran parallel to the city walls, and advanced towards the Gate of St George. The air rippled with the rhythmic sound of chinking mail and armour, at a pace which balanced speed against exhausting themselves before they reached their destination.

Edward nodded to Owen and a few knights carrying crossbows. They peeled off from the phalanx-like group and began to take a position on the roof of a hut, at the foot of the wall. The Englishman knew that they needed to overwhelm the enemy and open the gates, before support arrived and they were overwhelmed themselves.

The initial response of the Turkish soldiers at the gate was to just squint and take in the vague silhouette of men coming towards them. Were they fellow soldiers from the garrison, here to relieve them? Were they late-night revellers, celebrating the start of the crusaders' retreat?

But the truth soon dawned on them, like a hammer blow. The enemy had somehow infiltrated the city. A collective shudder of shock and disbelief infected the Antiochenes. Shouts ripped through the night air, like flesh being torn from bone. Cups and plates of food were thrown down. Spears were grasped. Pieces of armour were reached for and half strapped on. Guards who were asleep woke-up. Those who were awake leapt to their feet. Orders were issued to form up, by the two officers leading contingents of soldiers charged with guarding the gate. One of the captains of the watch bellowed up to the men on the ramparts. They were told to sound the alarm. For so long their evenings had been uneventful. The Franks had been kept at arm's length. But not tonight.

As when a horse breaks from a trot into the gallop, the knights, once they witnessed their enemy rousing themselves, charged. Swords were drawn. Edward heard the whistle of missiles over his head, as Owen and others unleashed their arrows and quarrels. A number hit their mark. First blood to the crusaders. The sound of individual steps slapping upon flagstones became one long din, like individual raindrops turning into a downpour.

The pilgrims broke into three groups. One, led by Fulk of Chartres, attacked the Turkish guards to the left of the gates. Edward was at the vanguard of the troops which engaged the soldiers on the right. Hugh commanded the remaining knights, tasking himself with opening the heavily barred entrance.

The force of armoured knights slammed into the lines of their wavering opponents, like a wave crashing against a rickety pier. War cries littered the air, like sparks flying off two great pieces of flint.

Fulk carried a large shield, with more than one dint and dent across its surface, and a gore-strewn mace. The brutal knight punched, kicked, barged, butted and swung his weapon against his foes. He would have been willing to bite ears and noses, given the chance. His nostrils were as flared as a charging bull. His wolfish grin had turned into a spittle-filled snarl. He put himself at the heart of the melee, goading or terrorising the enemy – and inspiring his fellow knights, whipping them into a similar violent frenzy.

Edward swatted away the tip of a Turkish spear and moved inside to plunge his sword into an enemy's stomach. He stuck out an elbow to fend off another assailant, breaking his nose. Blood curdling screams embroidered the air in front of him. Screams slashed his ears too, from behind, as a couple of men on the walls above threw spears into a brace of knights behind the Englishman. The guards manning the walls remained there, either feeling too helpless or scared to join their comrades fighting below.

Hugh attempted to bring order to chaos, mustering his men to heave off the bar across the door with their shoulders. An iron bolt, as stubborn as a harridan, also secured the gates. But a trio of knights descended upon it and either prised off the lock or smashed it with their heavy axes.

Captains were targeted, to leave the enemy leaderless. Edward was happy to provide his opponents with an excuse to rout and retreat. A handful of guards tried to surrender, but they were cut down without pause or remorse. The crusaders' blood was up, bubbling over. The knights, professional soldiers, could finally prove their quality against the citizen soldiers – made up of fishmongers, tailors, tanners and barbers.

Bells continued to clang overhead. Panicked shouts swirled around them, like leaves in a crosswind, as the Turks looked to call for reinforcements. But the knights would be reinforced first.

The gates were stiff, having been closed for so long. But they were not stiff enough.

As soon as Bohemond had heard the bells ring out from the watchtowers he ordered his men to advance, gambling that his company of knights would complete their mission.

His gamble paid off. The army knew that this would be their first and last chance to take the accursed city. The enemy had taunted them, from their ramparts, for months. It is easy to be brave behind walls.

A rasping cry of "Allahu Akbar" went up, but it was soon drowned out by the thunderous refrain of, "God wills it!"

God and hate fuelled the crusaders' advance. Hate fomented over six months. Six months of disease, starvation and close companions dying. But now the gates to the city were finally open.

Blood called for blood. The crusaders found extra strength and speed to assault their enemies, eating up the ground in front of them. The Turks were caught between the knights inside the city and Bohemond's ravenous troops. God was with them. The infidels scattered, like ashes in a breeze, when they realised that all was lost. Fulk kicked the ankles of a retreating guard, who had swapped sentry duties with his cousin for the evening. The knight then bludgeoned the floored Turk to death with several blows to his head. An unholy, shrill gurgle emanated from one of the Antiochenes manning the battlements as an arrow slashed through his nose and left eye. Owen took great pride in being able to shoot more prolifically – and accurately – than the crossbowmen standing next to him. The torrent of arrows and quarrels raining down on the guards prevented them from mobilising themselves properly, in order to rain missiles down on the ungodly invaders.

Corpses were trodden on, like weeds, as Bohemond's army entered the city. He positioned himself at the vanguard of his force – at the tip of the spear point. Occasionally he glanced back, to ensure that his bannerman was close. To stake his claim to the city.

Bugles were sounded, to signal to Godfrey's army, concealed under the cover of darkness outside the city to advance. Godfrey briefly wondered if the horns at the walls of Jericho sounded similar. Bohemond issued the order for part of his company to advance and open the gate. He would also muster a force to attack the citadel. Not only did he need to be wary of Raymond occupying the fortification, but he couldn't afford the Turks to possess it either. An intelligence report cited that the citadel was furnished with its own water cistern and generously provisioned. "We are more likely to entice a snail out of its shell than expel the Turks from their fortress, if they garrison it properly," Bohemond warned his men.

Bohemond was pleased to see Hugh alive and the two men greeted one another enthusiastically. The prince noticed that blood freckled his friend's face. But it was fine. It was the blood of their foes.

There would be little respite, however - and they dare not celebrate yet. The night would be long. Already a contingent of armed citizens and soldiers were forming up at the end of the street, carrying spears, cudgels and kitchen knives. Their foreign tongues were doubtless spitting out curses, rather than declarations of surrender. Bohemond instructed a group of troops, fresh and eager to bloody their swords, to form up and charge the enemy. Just as he was doing so however a commotion ensued amongst the gathering Turks, as they were attacked from behind by, as Bohemond would soon discover, a mob of Christians and Armenians native to the city. They wanted to punish their persecutors, as well as declare themselves allies of the crusaders. They would fight with them, rather than against them.

Godfrey's army entered the city as did Raymond's. They flowed through the gates and streets, like the Orontes bursting its banks. As when a drunk will spill his wine cup and clumsily try to scoop up the dregs to put back into the vessel, the Turks could not repel the enemy pouring through the city. The crusaders were possessed, by God or the Devil, as fiery eyed as the stars.

The garrison owned the numbers to engage and potentially expel the invaders, but they lacked the organisation and leadership. Yaghi Siyan woke to a nightmare. On hearing the news that the westerners were inside the walls the terrified governor chose flight over fight. He gathered up certain portable valuables and, accompanied by his personal bodyguard, Siyan escaped through the Iron Gate, leaving the Antiochenes to their fate, uttering all manner of curses at Kerbogha for not arriving earlier.

As Siyan glanced back at the city, having used his mount to barge through the throng of other departing citizens, he couldn't help but notice the growing plumes of smoke, entwined like rope, scarring the black, velvety night.

Siyan's son, Shams ad-Daulah, displayed more courage and initiative than his father, however – and not only because he couldn't display any less. He collected what troops he could find and ascended the slopes of Mount Silphius to secure the citadel. Holding the fortress could serve as a rallying point for the rest of the city, or provide a base to counterattack from, once Kerbogha's army engaged the perfidious infidels.

Thomas peered out of the window, at the ladder. Bohemond had nicknamed it "Jakob's Ladder" earlier.

"And once you scale it later the battle might be akin to a contest with God. But I have faith you will prevail. Because you will have to."

The youth thought how he could easily climb down and venture back to the camp. Many in Bohemond's army already considered the non-combatant to be a coward. Thomas felt like he was going to be sick. He had just come back from surveying the city from the battlements. Antioch was being put to the sword – and the torch. Flames were beginning to crackle through the gelid air. He felt little pride or a sense of glory when he spied Bohemond's banner through a pall of smoke. Adhemar had advised the Englishman not to put himself in danger, during the assault.

"Save yourself," the bishop remarked.

Adhemar's words briefly sounded like a siren song, enticing him to return to safety. People would forgive him for his actions. Yet Thomas couldn't forgive himself, nor should God forgive him, should he abandon the woman he had vowed to save. A promise is a promise. Even if his friend was acting dishonourably, or if Edward was dead, Thomas couldn't be dissuaded from his course. Tonight must witness at least one act of chivalry, he determined. The Englishman whispered the name, "Yeva", as he had once lovingly whispered the word "Jerusalem".

Thomas descended the steps of the tower rather than use the ladder. An acrid smell of smoke, like sulphur, filled his nostrils. He heard the screams of people dying, being slaughtered, in the distance. But the screams were getting closer. The scribe briefly closed his eyes and pictured the map of the city. Yeva's house wasn't as close as he would have liked. But every journey starts with a first step. Thomas set off whilst clasping his sword, although he was unsure how useful it would be if he drew it.

Dawn was breaking, bleeding light like an open wound.

The Turks had sowed the seed. Now they were reaping the whirlwind, Raymond of Toulouse judged as he observed his men execute another enemy officer, by cleaving his head from his body. The tang of blood and smoke were as welcome as the finest perfume to the soldier.

Godfrey's men and the Christian inhabitants of the city opened the Bridge Gate, which Raymond's army stormed through. His company fought with skill and savagery as they swiftly overcame Turkish resistance. It was butchery, rather than a battle. Bodies were dragged or kicked to the kerb. The flagstones were slick with blood.

Raymond nodded in satisfaction as Henri reported how his knights had secured the nearby Palace of Antioch. "No prisoners," he had instructed, before the attack. The prince wondered if his wife might finally forgive him, should he install her in the palace like a queen. But even more than the palace Raymond wanted to capture the strategic prize of the city's citadel. Raymond gave the order for Henri to lead as large a unit as he saw fit to capture the fortress – before Bohemond could.

"Do what you have to do," Raymond ordered, in response to his lieutenant asking what he should do, should he encounter Bohemond's men. The Frank had already noted how his rival's army hadn't helped open the Bridge Gate. Had Bohemond's plan been to keep Raymond's forces outside the city, whilst the Norman had free reign to procure all of Antioch's assets? "If Bohemond can break his promise to the Emperor, I can break my promise to him."

Death and dishonour were legion, spreading throughout Antioch like fire.

Screams pierced the night like sharpened lances but Bohemond's heart was armoured against such sounds. He could not now stop the slaughter or looting, even if he wished to do so. The screams were now emanating from women, as well as soldiers. To the victor, the spoils, the commander would have argued.

Bohemond's stentorian voice rose above the background noise. In order to further cement his claim to the city, the prince gave an order to find and apprehend Antioch's governor. His plan was to commit Siyan to signing the city – and its treasury - over to him. Bohemond might need his young scribe to help draft the decree.

"It's time to fetch Thomas. I may have need of him," the Norman remarked to Edward.

"I'll bring him here," the Englishman dutifully replied.

But it was easier said than done. When Edward returned to the room near the watchtower, he only found Firuz, clutching his chest of gold, and his two attendants. Thomas had taught the Armenian a few words of English, in case his countryman returned.

"He find Yeva," Firuz exclaimed, repeatedly, pointing downstairs.

"Bloody holy fool!" Edward pronounced, to the Armenian, himself or the world – whilst kicking a cup on the floor against the wall. His stomach lurched, imagining Thomas making his way through the volatile city. He was as good as dead, Edward thought. The knight could have returned to Bohemond and explained that Thomas had disappeared. But he didn't.

Edward stood at the foot of the watchtower, first glancing up the street which would lead him back to safety. And then he surveyed the route which would take him to the city's interior.

The wind chilled his sweat-glazed cheeks. His hair was matted with gore. He had jarred his knee during the skirmish at the Gate of St George and blood seeped from a wound in his thigh, from a Turkish leaf-shaped blade. He felt his strength ebbing away with the blood loss. His throat was as dry as the deserts he'd crossed. Water would have been good. Ale better.

Edward didn't quite know where he was going. Having not memorised the map Thomas had drawn up, he prayed to God to direct him. The soldier had to have faith, as he turned into a narrow street littered with corpses and puddles of blood. Buildings seemed to be leaning over him, as if they were about to collapse. But enough light seeped in. The bodies were contorted. Mangled. Skulls were staved in. Eyes were still open – piteous or accusatory. Flies started to congregate over glistening wounds. A couple of crusaders lay, like an island, in a sea of dead Turks. It was difficult to tell where the red crosses on their shoulders ended and the blood began.

War cries and the clash at arms still vaunted upwards and across Antioch, like the plumes of smoke. The pilgrims were in the ascendency, however. Turkish soldiers were dying or retreating. A few streets later Edward encountered a couple of crusaders exiting a house. The first was wiping his dagger on his sleeve, the second was fastening his britches and belt – and wiping the saliva from his mouth with the back of his hand.

"We were just having some fun. Sorry, we ended her. She screamed too much. The bitch had plenty of fight in her, but no money in her purse," the swarthy Frank remarked.

Edward pictured Emma being assaulted and the thought flashed through his mind that he should skewer the rapist. End him. Save others. But another half a dozen soldiers stumbled out of the house. Edward couldn't take them all on. He couldn't protect Thomas or Yeva if he was dead.

"Your orders are to travel back to the Gate of St George," Edward said, flatly.

"We still haven't got our dues," the soldier, who had wiped his dagger clean, asserted. He was keen to loot – and have as much fun as possible – for as long as possible.

"If you don't return to Bohemond then you risk him giving you what he thinks you're due," Edward warned. "I've heard that Fulk has already punished a number of men who defied orders," he added, lying, planting a seed a terror in their minds.

The threat of earning Bohemond and Fulk's displeasure brought the infantrymen into line. They may have mumbled certain grievances, but they started to make their way back, away from where they could murder, pilfer and rape.

Edward condemned himself as a holy fool, for continuing to endanger himself and search for Thomas. He walked on – witnessing more than a few soldiers coming out of shops and houses, carrying all manner of goods, like lines of pack animals. The knight also observed plenty of Turks, carrying children or their most valued possessions, running away from the fighting. Edward often concealed himself in doorways. Partly he didn't want to be attacked by any Antiochene – and partly he didn't want to unduly scare them. For the past year the word "Turk" had been synonymous with the word "enemy". But now he considered some of them to be victims. The veteran soldier had taken part in more than one sacking before. But he was increasingly viewing this one through fresh eyes.

Along with the Antiochenes, Edward spotted hordes of Franks sweeping through the streets. He suspected that many were being ordered to attack the citadel. Each prince knew the strategic value of capturing the fortress. The Englishman sometimes paused to take in groups or individual crusaders in the half light, in the hope of locating his countryman. But it was like trying to find a needle in a haystack. Edward reasoned that he could spend a month wending his through the criss-crossing streets and still not encounter the youth. But he had to still try. The knight would not abandon his friend, as Thomas would not abandon the girl.

15.

Thomas moved through the dim city streets as swiftly as possible, avoiding both fellow crusaders and Antiochenes alike. At one point he considered that he might have died and turned into a ghost, as people looked his way but didn't necessarily see him. Bohemond had once half-joked that he should turn his scribe into a spy, as no one seemed to notice when he came and went. Even when the darkness began to melt away like ice and a milky, morning light dripped through the city, Thomas remained unseen.

There was more than one instance when he took the long way around, to avoid detection. He was sometimes frozen in fear too and needed to collect himself. Thomas encountered dozens of blood-strewn corpses, in the wake of soldiers pillaging and abducting women. He vomited on viewing and smelling the charred remains of a young girl. Severed ears and hands littered the ground. He considered the Franks to be similar to a plague of Egypt. Locusts. The gates of Hell had been opened. Was Bohemond of the Devil's party? The student imagined that his journey across the city resembled Virgil's descent into the underworld. Thomas witnessed sights he wished to un-see. A group of soldiers, carrying lances, amused themselves by each stabbing an elderly Turk. Their laughter drowned out his groans of agony as they drew blood with each strike, albeit they ensured that they didn't kill their victim, lest they end their sport too prematurely.

He felt shame and then contempt in relation to his Christian brothers. There was nothing holy about their crusade tonight. They wouldn't be able to ever wash out the stain of sin, as their clothes would forever smell of smoke. He tried to recall a passage from the Bible, or from the Song of Roland, to gift himself some consolation – but his mind was blank. Burnt out. For once Thomas craved wine and ale over water and milk. His throat was sore, like he had swallowed a cup of hot iron filings. His legs frequently felt like they might give way, as if he had been running over cobblestones. The pilgrim's faith began to ebb away, like the blood and ordure running down the gutter.

How could God allow such heinous crimes in His name? If this was all part of some grand plan, it was a plan that he wanted no part of. Edward's words chimed in Thomas' ears, that "the world is an unpleasant place, filled with unpleasant people." Even if the Christian devoted his life to uttering one long, devout prayer it still wouldn't make a jot of difference in trying to redeem the wickedness in the world. It would be easier to extract the darkness out of the night, than remove sin from the world.

But Thomas believed that if he somehow saved Yeva, all would be redeemed. Honour would be satisfied. He still believed that the beautiful, virtuous woman was waiting for him. He would keep his word. Yet the Englishman's heart pounded with apprehension, as well as ardour, as he thought how Yeva might not be alone when he found her. His skin prickled. What if her husband were present? What if she was being held captive or being assaulted by a pack of soldiers? What could he do to stop them? Even if he could summon the courage to draw his sword and attack them, they would easily disarm and slay him.

But he would save her, Thomas resolutely told himself.

God wills it.

When Edward first heard the cry, as he strode down through the alley, leaning forward as if he were walking against a headwind, he didn't think to pause. He had grown inured, immune, to such sounds – having heard them during past campaigns. If truth be told he had occasionally been the cause of such screams.

But the knight now halted – and tacked back towards the desperate howls of terror and grief, from the woman, slicing through the vented shutters of the house. He also heard a child, bawling, too. The knight pictured Emma being assaulted again. The cries of the child would have been similar to his own, after his parents had been murdered by Norman soldiers all those years ago.

Edward walked through the door, which remained ajar from being forced open. Even in a foreign tongue, begging still sounded like begging. As the knight entered the room he wondered if the woman was pleading for her own life or her child's. The chamber, which served as both a kitchen and dining area, had been ransacked, like it had been caught up in a tempest.

The first Frank, Peter, who seemed little older than Thomas, was holding a knife to the boy's throat (the child was trembling like a leaf, blubbing, uttering the same word over and over again). The soldier was gaunt – as lean as a tent pole. He no longer filled out his hauberk. A Y-shaped scar, like a bird's footprint, branded his left cheek. He stared at Edward, his mouth agape, either shocked or seething that he had been disturbed. The second soldier, standing over the woman, was older – grizzled. He was in the process of transferring the contents of a jewellery box into a leather bag. The crusader, Bruno, was a former tavern owner from Caen. What profits he didn't gamble away, he drank. The pilgrimage offered the debtor a chance to earn some booty and return him to his station.

The distressed woman, Sophia, was crouched in a corner. Tears both fresh and drying, marked her quivering countenance.

The front of her dress had been torn and she endeavoured to cover her exposed breasts. Blood tricked down her chin, from her split bottom lip, from where Bruno had punched her, to stop the woman screaming. The small wound looked like a stem had been cut lengthways, below a flower. Edward later lamented that the woman had probably been a beauty before the siege – although there were no guarantees that she would be attractive again. Life had gotten its claws into her, carving worry lines into her smooth semblance. The Englishman's heart went out to the poor woman, albeit his focus needed to turn towards her tormentors.

As bellicose as Edward was feeling he decided to sheath his sword, to ease the tension and air of threat and violence. As he did so the young Frank removed his blade from the boy's neck.

"What do you want?" Bruno asked, or rather demanded. Tonight was their God-given reward, the soldier believed, for what they had endured these past months. The enemy deserved any and every punishment a prince or pilgrim could mete out. All would be lawful. Just.

"I want you to leave this place," Edward remarked, unequivocally. Unblinking. Obsidian-hard. He looked like he wanted to kill the bully and rapist. Because he did. Although the scenario was two against one, Edward didn't remotely feel like he was outnumbered.

"Find your own woman and chattel. There are plenty of houses to choose from. The city is ours."

A pregnant pause ensued, that was likely to give birth to conflict. Edward read his opponent. The Frank was calculating how he could kill the knight with impunity. There would be no witnesses. Bruno also eyed Edward up, surveying the quality of his boots and weaponry.

"Leave – and live," the Englishman replied, his voice akin to a block of iron.

"Ha! You think you are in a position to threaten me or give me orders?" the man-at-arms countered, screwing up his face as if he were breathing in vapours from a sewer. You want to play the chivalrous knight? This is not the time or place to do so. Chivalry's dead."

"I'm not sure whether chivalry's dead or not, but you will be if you don't depart. You can keep the jewels."

Bruno let out a burst of scornful laughter, turning to his companion as he did so. Whether Edward considered himself chivalrous or not, he knew how to fight in an unchivalrous way. Whilst the old soldier's attention was diverted, Edward quickly drew the dagger from the back of his belt and threw it into the Frank's chest. He retrieved his second knife and launched it into his torso too, for good measure. Bruno stumbled backwards, losing his footing on some of the furniture he had smashed, blacking out and eventually bleeding out.

Sophia screamed. The sound resembled a gauntlet scraping, screeching, down a pane of glass. She moved towards her child. The boy scrambled away from his captor and reached for her in return. The mother clutched the boy to her chest and turned her back to the soldiers, shielding him from the barbaric westerners.

Peter drew his slightly bent sword, having still not recovered from his friend's sudden defeat. His head swivelled left and right, searching for an escape route which didn't exist. Edward moved towards him, cornering the Frank like prey. Peter had killed a couple of Turks before, as they lay wounded after a skirmish. He had also murdered a young woman before, after he had raped her. But he had never defeated an opponent in combat.

The petrified youth swung his weapon, with little conviction or skill. Edward's attack was defter and more determined. The knight motioned to deliver an attack at a high angle. Peter held his sword aloft to block it, but as he did so Edward altered the direction of the stroke. The sharp tip of his blade sliced through his woollen shirt once, from right to left – and then left to right. Eviscerating the rapist. His intestines began to peek out of his shirt. Peter dropped his weapon, clanging like a death knell. Shortly afterwards the Frank fell to the ground too – after Edward had stabbed him in the throat.

The knight wiped his blade on the corpse and then sheathed the well-crafted blade. Edward raised his gloved palms, to convey to the woman and child that he meant them no harm. The mother understandably appeared anxious still, fearing that the knight might finish off what others began. But she soon appreciated that the crusader wasn't any threat, as he retrieved her jewellery, placed it back into the box, left it next to her and took his leave.

Yeva was beautiful. Achingly so. As beautiful as Briseis, who Thomas pictured her as being like. Such beauty could inspire a man to believe in God. Her hair, as black and shiny as tar, hung down past her graceful shoulders. Her bronzed skin was as flawless as he had imagined it, during his frequent reveries. Her emerald eyes shone like the surface of the Orontes on a calm, summer's day. Her saffron coloured silk dress clung to her hourglass figure. Yeva was beautiful. But dead. Such beauty, defiled, could cause a man to doubt God.

A red, lily-shaped stain just beneath her breasts marked where the woman had been stabbed. Broken furniture, smashed plates and feathers, from where someone had slashed open the nearby sofa in hope of locating valuables, surrounded the woman. A waif-like man, presumably her husband, was dangling from a beam above her. His eyes were bulging, fit to explode, and his tongue was lolling out of his mouth. His face was lacerated, bloated and purple – like a burst grape. The soldiers had beaten the man to within an inch of his life, before hanging him.

Lemony sunshine scythed through the room, highlighting motes of dust, which danced around like flies. Thomas dropped to his knees, as though grief were a stone around his neck, weighing him down. He was nauseous, to the pit of his stomach, but couldn't quite be sick. His young face was creased up like an old man's, as if he was about to weep, but somehow the tears didn't fall. He was all cried out. Thomas felt both hollowed out and overstuffed with sorrow and rage. He wanted God to punish the guilty. He wanted to pray for vengeance, not mercy or forgiveness. He couldn't quite bring himself to pray, however, as much as he was on his knees. Any prayer would be in vain, like others.

Thomas adjusted the ripped skirt on Yeva's dress, to cover up her thighs and womanhood, as best as possible. Her skin was not quite as cold and pale as he imagined it would be, when he bent over and kissed her forehead. He had pictured himself kissing the young woman on her rosebud mouth beforehand, but he desisted from doing so now.

Could he have saved Yeva if he reached her earlier? He was too tired to blame himself or Edward. But he couldn't exonerate himself or Edward either. Honour couldn't be redeemed. He felt like his own life was, or should be, forfeit. If only he had remained in his village, instead of journeying to Cluny. If only he had stayed in Cluny, instead of travelling to Clermont. Thomas once believed that that day had been the making of him. But it had been his undoing.

The morning light initially hurt his eyes, but Edward was becoming accustomed to it. He would squint and scrutinise any figure resembling Thomas. It was bright enough to spot him. But he was nowhere to be seen. His friend could have perished from encountering fellow crusaders, caught up in their bloodlust, or he could have easily made the wrong turn and found himself on the end of a Turkish blade. If Thomas had died, Edward mused, then he would have ascended to Heaven.

He's in a better place, better even than a tavern in London or brothel in Constantinople perhaps.

And what if the next life wasn't Heaven, or Hell? What if there was nothing, darkness? His fate would still be worth envying, the soldier surmised. The world was an unpleasant place, filled with unpleasant people. Perhaps Thomas was too good, innocent, for this iniquitous world. Life is a cruel – or the cruellest - joke. The only way to endure was to laugh in the face of God's prank.

Edward glimpsed a small fountain at the end of a narrow alley. He remembered Thomas mentioning that Yeva's house was near to a small fountain. Perhaps he was close. Perhaps there was cause for hope.

The crossbow bolt struck him in the left buttock, as if an asp had leapt up and bitten the knight. A couple of moments later a second quarrel sliced through his right shoulder. The force of the blows both spun Edward around and knocked him to the ground.

Disorientated. Weakened. The injury to his posterior prevented Edward from getting to his feet. The wound to his shoulder meant that his right arm was tantamount to being lame. He still instinctively drew his dagger with his left hand, but he was unused to using it. He attempted to throw the blade at his advancing assailant, but the mail-clad Frank easily swatted the missile away with his broad sword. The English knight managed to draw his sword, but his opponent closed in and forced the weapon out of his weaker hand.

The pitiless Frank stood over his quarry, ready to deliver a killing blow. Edward didn't recognise the crusader. But he did recognise the figure standing next to him. Girard of Mortain.

The nobleman was marching through the city, buried in a crowd of soldiers that Raymond had ordered to surround the citadel. He wanted to help storm the fortress, to prove himself to his uncle – and hopefully smuggle out some riches concealed in the building. But when he observed his enemy from across a square, alone and vulnerable, he instructed Pierre to leave the group and accompany him. The two men, who had spent plenty of time together hunting, stalked a new prey. As much as Girard's blood was up, he knew he needed to be patient. They might only have an opportunity to shoot their crossbows once. The nobleman re-lived the feelings of shame and dishonour after his bout with the Englishman, to stoke the fire in his belly. He blamed the knight too for his uncle denuding him of his company and assets. Girard had dreamed of standing over his enemy, of being able to torture and kill the ignoble Englishman. His prayers had been answered.

The Norman wanted to savour the moment. He wanted the Englishman to beg for his life. To humiliate himself, as much as Girard had been humiliated. No matter how much the knight pleaded though, he would execute him. Slowly. Painfully. He noticed a dirty rag in the corner, which he thought he could use to gag Edward and silence his screams, while he tortured him. He would mutilate his victim's face, so the corpse couldn't be recognised. He would stab him in the groin, feet and thighs, as an experiment to measure how much pain was elicited in each area.

"You're going to die," Girard remarked, with relish. His triumphant smile wrapped itself around his face, lizard-like.

"Ain't we all?" Edward replied, wistfully, dribbling as he spoke. His eyes were half-closed. The lids were bruise-coloured. The knight was light-headed, like he was drunk. He was more weary than angry. Death was calling him. The light was growing dimmer. Rather than ask to be delivered himself, Edward prayed to God to keep Emma safe. He thought how, having saved the woman and child earlier in the evening, he was starting to be deserving of her love. He wondered if he might see his mother again, in the next life.

Edward recalled the words that Adhemar had marked in his Bible.

"Only the person who is put right with God through faith shall live."

He started to understand and appreciate what he had read. But was it too late?

The blade sluiced through flesh, scraped against bone and burst his heart. His eyes were momentarily stapled wide in agony and surprise. Pierre emitted a gasp, before he died, like he had just heard a salacious piece of gossip. Thomas had aimed the tip of his sword at the gap between where the Norman's mail shirt was strapped across his back. The scribe knew that he had to murder in cold blood, without any chivalric warning – else both Edward and himself would perish.

Whether through luck or God's providence Thomas had been walking past the mouth of the alleyway when the soldiers put their crossbows on the ground and approached his wounded countryman, their swords drawn.

Time stood still for a few moments as Thomas kept his sword lodged in Pierre and Girard stood dumb, incredulous. The nobleman had taken the scribe for a coward. The smile fell from his face, as abruptly as Pierre slumped to the ground, as Thomas withdrew his weapon.

Self-preservation, as much as any skill, compelled Thomas to raise his sword in time as Girard swung his blade. Thomas parried several times. The song of swords. The alley reverberated with a primal roar from the Norman. From seeing his friend die. From being a disappointing second son. From never being loved. From being mocked after his defeat to Edward. From his uncle treating him like a child. Rage blunted his technique and focus.

Thomas was forced backwards. He observed Edward, still on the ground behind Girard, dragging himself towards his sword – in order to then crawl towards his enemy and engage him. But he moved slowly, feebly. Should Girard turn around he would easily be able to slay his friend. Thomas knew he needed to defeat his opponent, else they would both be murdered.

Thou shalt kill.

The student remembered one of his first lessons with Edward. The knight tried to drill into Thomas a move to turn defence into attack.

Deflect and then strike.

Thomas re-positioned his feet, so he could move backwards and forwards more effectively. He glowered at the Norman (it was perhaps the first time the pilgrim had ever glowered), challenging him. Goading him. He deserved to die. He may have even been involved in Yeva's rape and murder - Thomas told himself.

The tips of their blades touched. Kissed.

Counterattack rather than attack.

Girard advanced, raising his sword, with the intention of bringing it down on the scribe's collarbone. Thomas was quick to react - quicker than his opponent expected - catching him unawares. Using all the might he could muster the Englishman deflected the attack – and then lunged forward, to bury the point of his weapon into one of the areas which Edward always advised. His throat. Girard's jaw moved up and down, spasming, as if he were chewing a tough piece of meat. He gurgled loudly, rather than roared, as he writhed on the floor.

Blood gushed from the wound, as freely as the nearby fountain sprayed water from its chipped spout.

Thomas trembled from shock too, initially. Blood stained his brow, like the mark of Cain. The sword point wavered over its scabbard. He had to clasp the tip and feed it in, to sheathe the glistening weapon. Edward looked up at his friend – and was going to exclaim that he didn't think that Thomas had it in him. But in some ways the holy fool was more of a knight - or what a knight should be - than anyone else he knew.

Both men offered each other a weak smile. But it was still a smile nonetheless.

"I couldn't save her," the scribe announced - as much to himself, as to the world or Edward. His voice croaked as he spoke. Thomas no longer appeared as innocent as he once did. Once a bone is broken, it can never be quite as strong again.

"You can't save everyone, Thomas," Edward replied, endeavouring to console his friend. "But take heart. You helped to save me."

16. Epilogue.

A yellow, wafer-like sun hung in the sapphire-blue sky. Petals of light were strewn across the shimmering surface of the Orontes. Nature was at peace, even if the world wasn't.

The fires were being extinguished, or they burned themselves out. The princes began to instil discipline again among their troops. There were also few houses left to loot, or women left alive to rape and slaughter.

Adhemar surveyed what had been a vibrant bazaar in the city. Instead of shoppers, the square was now populated by a mound of corpses. Bodies and limbs were tangled up with one another, like a fleshy briar patch. Ghoulish eyes upon ghoulish eyes, set above rictus after rictus, gazed out from the pyramid of the dead. The jelly from one woman's eye dripped down her cheek, like tears. There were scores of children among the macabre edifice. One was too many, the bishop judged.

"What message will our actions here send out to the world?" Adhemar remarked to Raymond, as the two men had stood on the battlements and gazed out across the devasted city.

"It will send out a message that we are a force to be reckoned with," the count replied, unapologetically. Proud.

Not everyone subscribed to Raymond's view, however. Adhemar shared a telling look with Godfrey, which conveyed how the Christian prince believed that the army had covered itself in shame, rather than glory. The bishop often took Godfrey's confession. Usually he would confess to various venial sins – and his penance would be to merely recite some prayers. But Adhemar wasn't quite sure how he, or God, could absolve Godfrey and others of the sins they were responsible for yesternight. Every crusader should examine his conscience, although the clergyman suspected that every man was probably examining the loot or food they stole.

Adhemar continued to traverse through the city. Even when he walked down some of the sloping streets, he felt like he was marching uphill. Discarded garments, not fit for pilfering, along with cutlery, crockery, heirlooms and swaddling clothes littered the streets. The dead lay on flagstones, like pieces of dung. The city smelled like a burial pit.

Eventually the bishop arrived at the Cathedral of St Peter. He wanted to restore and reconsecrate the church. It was a start.

The pilgrims occupying the camps outside of Antioch began to move into the city. Many wept in joy, believing that they had been delivered. The worst was now over, they mistakenly thought. Edward waited by the Gate of St George, for Emma. Bohemond had instructed his personal surgeon, Charles of Anjou, to attend to the Englishman. He stitched up his wounds and provided the knight with a cane, to help alleviate his temporary limp. The surgeon wiped the blood and grime from his patient's careworn countenance, to make him appear more presentable.

"I'm not sure whether to consider you lucky or not, given what your body has been through," Charles mused.

"Another battle, another scar," the knight replied, more sanguine than one might have expected. He would have shrugged his shoulders, if the gesture wouldn't have been so painful.

Remarkably Thomas was free from any injury, although some scars remain unseen. He certainly appeared ill. Drawn. There was a faraway look in his eyes, that Edward had recognised on many a soldier before. His young friend seemed distracted and, despite their victory, defeated.

"You look like hell, Thomas. But when you're going through hell, keep going," Edward advised.

As the two Englishmen made their way from the surgeon, towards the Gate of St George, they saw Fulk of Chartres striding towards them. The Norman had placed himself on the frontline throughout the evening. Bone and brain marked his mace. His clothes and countenance were awash with blood, like he had bathed in the stuff.

"He looks like Coriolanus," Thomas said, slightly aghast.

"I'm not sure I know who that is. Is he part of Raymond's company?"

The scribe let out a burst of laughter. Edward didn't quite know what his friend found amusing. The knight was just pleased that Thomas was laughing again.

Raymond's banner fluttered behind him, having been hoisted atop of the Palace of Antioch. Henri of Bayeux, who had typically fought well the night before, had just provided the prince with the butcher's bill. When his lieutenant reported that his nephew was among the dead, Raymond replied that he was "neither surprised nor saddened." Overall, the general was pleased with the limited losses. He still commanded the largest army. The Frank imagined that Bohemond would be pleased with his night's work too, as he glanced at his rival's banner, flying over the Gate of St George, and scrunched up his features in acrimony. But the Emperor and his army would be arriving soon. The Norman's claim to the city would come to nothing. He who laughs last, laughs longest.

I've outfoxed the son of Robert Guiscard.

Bohemond stood on the wall, close to the Tower of Two Sisters. The pilgrims below, on both sides of the wall, sometimes chanted his name and expressed their gratitude. The nobleman resisted playing to the crowd and remained imperious, regal. He was pleased, both for the people and his own ambitions, that he had saved the crusade. For now, at least.

The prince had recently finished convening with his ally, Firuz. He had left the Armenian with his gold and the news that the crusaders had "unwittingly" killed his brother during the assault. All the money in the world couldn't bring him back.

Nor would Yaghi Siyan be coming back. After the governor escaped, he was thrown from his horse. The deserter was abandoned by his men and left for dead. Siyan was discovered by an Armenian butcher, who swiftly cut off his head, with his wispy white beard still hanging from his chin - and brought the trophy home to Antioch.

It was a strange but welcome sight, viewing the sun-scorched plains of Antioch from the vantage point of the city, Bohemond considered. For how many nights had Yaghi Siyan's men stared out at the crusader camps and heaped curses of them? For how many nights would the Army of God man the walls and curse Kerbogha's forces?

The besiegers would soon become the besieged.

End Note.

Although *Siege* follows historic events and features key figures from history the book is primarily a work of fiction. Am hoping however that the novel will inspire some people to read about the real history behind the First Crusade. The job of a book is to compel a reader to pick up another book.

I can highly recommend the following: *The First Crusade: A New History*, by Thomas Asbridge; *The First Crusade and the Foundation of the Kingdom of Jerusalem*, by Stephen Runciman; *Crusaders*, by Dan Jones.

I would like to thank Sophie Ambler, for enthusing and informing me about some aspects of the First Crusade. I would also like to thank Rob Kemp for his support and work on the manuscript.

Siege is the first book in a planned trilogy set during the First Crusade. Should you have enjoyed the book please do get in touch, as would welcome relevant feedback in light of writing future titles in the series. Please do contact me too if you have enjoyed any past books I've written. I can be reached at richard@sharpebooks.com and @rforemanauthor on twitter.

Edward Kemp and Thomas Devin will return in *Besieged*.

Richard Foreman

*

Printed by Amazon Italia Logistica S.r.l.
Torrazza Piemonte (TO), Italy